1-10-06

HAIL TO THE CHIEF

an 87th Precinct mystery

**Center Point
Large Print**

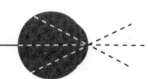

**This Large Print Book carries the
Seal of Approval of N.A.V.H.**

HAIL TO THE CHIEF
an 87th Precinct mystery

ED MCBAIN

CENTER POINT PUBLISHING
THORNDIKE, MAINE

This is for
Sylvia and Don Bunt

The city in these pages is imaginary.
The people, the places, are all fictitious.
Only the police routine is based on
established investigatory technique.

This Center Point Large Print edition
is published in the year 2003 by arrangement with
HUI Corp. c/o Gelfman Schneider Literary Agency.

The text of this Large Print edition is unabridged. In other
aspects, this book may vary from the original edition. Printed in
Thailand. Set in 16-point Times New Roman type by
Bill Coskrey and Gary Socquet.

ISBN 1-58547-307-3

Library of Congress Cataloging-in-Publication Data.

McBain, Ed, 1926-
    Hail to the chief : an 87th Precinct mystery / Ed McBain.--Center Point large print ed.
    p. cm.
    ISBN 1-58547-307-3 (lib. bdg. : alk. paper)
    1. 87th Precinct (Imaginary place)--Fiction. 2. Police--United States--Fiction.
3. Large type books. I. Title.

PS3515.U585 H3 2003
813'.54--dc21

                                                              2002041275

1

THEY found the bodies in an open ditch on the northernmost extreme of the 87th Precinct. The telephone company had torn up the street early the morning before, to get at the underground cables. The repairmen finished the job by nightfall, when the temperature dropped below freezing. They had covered the ditch with temporary wooden planking, and had erected blinking barriers around the excavation, to keep motorists away from the long, narrow, covered trench in the earth. Someone had ripped up the planking and dropped the six bodies into the ditch. Two radio-car cops, on routine patrol near the boat basin, spotted the ripped-up sections of planking and flashed their torches into the excavation. The date was January the sixth. The time was three in the morning. By three-ten, Detectives Steve Carella and Bertram Kling were on the scene.

The bottom of the ditch was a maze of electrical and telephone cables. Water had seeped into the ditch, combining with the freshly spaded earth to form a quagmire which had frozen over at nightfall, so that the cables now seemed embedded in brown plastic. The six bodies were lying in angular confusion on top of the mud-colored ice. There was another color staining the ice. The color was blood. The bodies were naked. Their nakedness made the night seem even colder than it was. Carella, wearing a fleece-lined leather jacket, brown woolen gloves, and earmuffs, looked down into the ditch. Kling was fanning the beam of his flashlight over the bodies. Ten feet from where they were standing, two radio motor patrol cars blinked their revolving red lights into the night. Now that the detectives were here, the patrolmen had gone back into the cars to keep warm.

There were three men, two young girls, and a baby in the ditch. The baby was clutched in the arms of one of the girls. Carella did not turn away until he saw the baby. Up to that moment, this was another homicide, grislier than most, but you don't turn away from any of them unless you're going to turn away from all of them. The sight of the dead baby caused a short, sharp stab of pain somewhere behind his eyes. He said "Jesus" as he turned away from the ditch, and behind him he heard Kling catch his breath, and knew that he had seen the baby, too. Kling turned off the flashlight. They moved farther away from the ditch, as though proximity to it might in some way be contaminating. Their vapored breaths feathered out onto the air. In the distance they heard a police siren. For several moments neither of the cops said anything. Kling, gloveless and hatless, his blond hair blowing in the wind, put the flashlight under his arm, and immediately thrust both hands into the pockets of his car coat. His shoulders hunched, his chin ducked into his collar, he said, very softly, "It reminds me of the bookshop," and for a moment Carella did not know what he meant. And then, of course, he recalled a day in October, thirteen years ago, when he and Kling had stepped into a bookshop on Culver Avenue and found four dead bodies on the floor. One of the victims had been Kling's girl friend, Claire Townsend.

Physically, Kling had not changed very much in those thirteen years—oh, perhaps around the eyes a little, a weariness around the eyes. But he still looked quite young, the blond hair and hazel eyes combining with a clean-shaven, well-scrubbed sort of face that never seemed to age. Carella looked into that face now, studying the eyes, trying to fathom whether Kling's memory of the bookshop was as vivid as his own, or whether he had learned to deal with that long-ago pain by blocking it out, pretending it had never happened. Jesus, that day. Jesus, when he had called the lieutenant and told him to get over there right away because Kling's girl had been killed—Jesus, the way he had stammered on the telephone, almost unable to get the words past his lips.

Both men looked up at the sound of the approaching siren. An unmarked car pulled to the curb, its tailpipe throwing a blue-gray ghost into the air. The two detectives who stepped out of the car were dressed almost identically, each wearing black overcoat and gray fedora, black leather gloves, blue woolen muffler. Both of the men were sturdily built, with wide shoulders and beefy chests and thighs, craggy faces and eyes that had seen it all, seen it all: Monoghan and Monroe from Homicide, the Tweedledum and Tweedledee of criminal investigation.

"Well, well, you guys never sleep, do you?" Monoghan said.

"They're always awake," Monroe said.

"Always got a body or two for us in the middle of the night, don't you?" Monoghan said.

"Few more than that this time," Carella said.

"Yeah?" Monroe said.

"Where are they?" Monoghan asked.

"Over in the ditch there," Kling said.

They watched as the two Homicide detectives walked over toward the ditch. In the city for which these men worked, the appearance of Homicide cops at the scene of a murder was mandatory, even though the subsequent investigation was handled by the precinct detectives catching the squeal. Carella and Kling looked upon the cops from Homicide as a nuisance. In rare instances, and presumably because they were "specialists," they would sometimes come up with an idea that helped expedite the solution of a case. More often than that, however—rather like eye, ear, nose, and throat men advising a general practitioner that his patient was deaf, dumb, blind, and suffering besides from sinus trouble and laryngitis—they merely stated the obvious, confused the issues, and demanded reports in triplicate for their own department. Homicide cops, in short, were pains in the ass to detectives actually in the field trying to solve murder cases. Monoghan and Monroe were *supreme* pains in the ass.

"Look at this, willya?" Monoghan said, throwing the beam of his flashlight into the ditch.

"Must be at least six of them down there," Monroe said.

"Half a dozen, anyway," Monoghan said.

"What's that?" Monroe said. "A baby?"

"An infant," Monoghan said.

"Now I seen everything," Monroe said.

"I seen one worse than this," Monoghan said.

"Worse than a baby in a ditch in the middle of January on a night you could freeze your balls off?"

"Much worse," Monoghan said. "This was back in the fifties, I was still working out of the Eight-Three, that's one hell of a precinct, I can tell you."

"Oh, don't I *know* it," Monroe said. "That's the precinct where Ralphie Donatello got shot in the back with an African blowgun."

"A poison dart," Monoghan said.

"Yeah," Monroe said.

"That was during my time," Monoghan said. "I used to know Ralphie. He was a damn good cop. Can you imagine? A poison dart?"

"Truth is stranger than fiction," Monroe said, and shook his head.

"Anyway, this case I was on, there were fourteen old ladies buried in the basement. Four*teen* of them. Made Bluebeard look like a kid who didn't even shave yet. Four*teen* of them."

"How old?"

"Old. Seventy, eighty, like that. Guy stabbed them all and put them in the basement. The way we found the bodies was a plumber came in to work on some pipes. *That* was worse than this. Much worse."

"Yeah, but these are all young kids," Monroe said, leaning over the edge of the ditch for a better look.

"Not so young. The guy with the beard looks

9

twenty-four, twenty-five."

"Yeah, but the others look like teen-agers."

"The girls especially."

"Fourteen or fifteen, huh?"

"Little older maybe."

"Sixteen?"

"Seventeen, maybe."

"Nice tits on the black one," Monroe said.

"Yeah," Monoghan said appreciatively.

Some distance away from the two Homicide cops, Carella and Kling stood silently, their hands in the pockets of their coats. Carella was a tall man, but his head was ducked and his shoulders were hunched against the cold, and he seemed shorter now than he actually was. In addition, his face was pinched and pale, his downward-slanting brown eyes (which often lent an Oriental cast to his features) were watering, his lips were chapped, he had cut himself shaving, and he looked like a wino searching for a warm doorway. So whereas he normally gave the appearance of a man whose tremendous strength was camouflaged in the deceptively trim body of an athlete, tonight he looked sniveling and scrawny in his leather jacket. He was cold, and he didn't like two hairbags from Homicide discussing those bodies so casually. He took out his handkerchief and blew his nose. Neither the lab technician nor the medical examiner had yet arrived. It was going to be a long night.

Monoghan and Monroe were walking back. "Got yourselves a regular massacre this time," Monoghan said.

"Little Big Horn," Monroe said.

"My Lai," Monoghan said.

"Must be three or four bullet holes in each and every one of them."

"Even the baby."

"The infant."

"Not a stitch on any of them."

"Must've plugged them someplace else and then dragged them over here to dump 'em."

"Probably heading for the river."

"A watery grave."

"Burial at sea."

"Spotted the ditch and decided to get rid of them here."

"Unless he brought 'em here bare-assed and shot them on the spot."

"That sounds dubious," Monroe said.

"But possible."

"But far-fetched."

"Who knows?" Monoghan said, and shrugged.

"Anyway, you guys got your work cut out for you," Monroe said. "Without no clothes on them, you'll even have trouble getting a positive identification."

"Unless a basketball team is reported missing," Monoghan said.

"Only *five* people on a basketball team," Monroe said. "There's six in the ditch."

"Maybe the baby was a mascot or something."

Monroe shrugged. He turned to Carella and said, "Keep us informed, huh?"

"Sure," Carella said.

"You don't mind if we split before the M.E. arrives, do you? It's colder'n an Eskimo's ass out here."

"We'll let you know what he says," Carella said.

"Anyway, he won't come up with no surprises," Monoghan said. "They were shot, and from the looks of the burn marks, it was at close range."

"Must be some nut," Monroe said.

"Some madman."

"Some deranged person. Who else would put three bullet holes in a baby?"

"Three or four," Monoghan corrected.

"Yeah, three or four," Monroe said.

"It's *got* to be some madman."

The two Homicide cops went back to their car. Carella and Kling watched while they drove off. One of the radio motor patrolmen had gone out for coffee, and he came back with two containers for Carella and Kling. In the empty hours of the night, steam rising from the open containers, steam rising too from the manhole covers in the black asphalt street, they sipped at the hot coffee and waited for the rest of the investigative team to arrive. On the river, a tugboat's horn bleated briefly, and then was silent. It sounded as though someone had hit the button by accident.

Carella and Kling waited.

In a little while, if they didn't freeze first, they would have information from the laboratory technician and the medical examiner.

THERE were no bullets in any of the bodies, nor were there bullets or cartridge cases in the ditch where the bodies had been found. It had to be assumed (as Monoghan, or Monroe, or both had stated) that the victims had been shot elsewhere and then transported to the lonely side street off the River Harb. The medical examiner ascertained that multiple gunshot wounds had been the cause of death in each case, but he would not go out on a limb concerning the post-mortem interval. Body heat and the absence or presence of rigor mortis are determining factors in establishing the moment of death, and since the stiffs found in the ditch were literally stiff, having been put on ice (so to speak), the M.E. was simply unwilling to even *guess* at how long the victims had been dead. Nor could he tell from the size or shape of the wounds whether the murder weapon had been a rifle or a pistol, although he *was* willing to venture (in keeping with the prognostications of those master criminologists Monoghan and Monroe) that judging from the burn marks, the victims had been shot at close range.

The man from the Photo Unit photographed the ditch and the vicinity surrounding the ditch, and the bodies lying in the ditch, and the buildings directly opposite the ditch, and then (after the position of the bodies had been marked) he photographed the empty ditch itself. This last had nothing to do with solving the crime. It had only to do with getting a conviction once the murderer was found, since very often dead bodies in photographs of a murder scene were considered objectionable or highly inflammatory to a jury and were not permitted in court.

Carella and Kling had sketched the murder scene

before the M.E. arrived, and had written an accurate description of it as well, including weather conditions, visibility, and illumination provided by street lamps or other light sources. Since the bodies were all naked, and since an examination of hands would be necessary for identification purposes, they covered the victims' hands with plastic bags the moment the M.E. finished his examination. The bodies were carried off to the morgue in two separate ambulances, and Kling, Carella, and the lab technician searched the ditch and the street for possible footprints, tire marks, weapons, *anything* that might help them to determine how the thing had happened and who had done it. They then made a record of the license plates on all of the parked autos near the scene of the crime, and went back to the squadroom.

The photographer, the lab technician, and the medical examiner were just beginning.

FINGERPRINTING a dead body (clothed or naked) is no more difficult than fingerprinting a live one. Once you get the fingers unclenched, the rest is duck soup. Taking a picture of a dead body is quite another cup of tea. Dead bodies have a tendency to look dead, you see. If the eyes are open (and there is nothing scarier than walking into a room and finding a dead person staring up at the ceiling), they retreat into their sockets and develop a grayish film over the eyeballs. If the eyes are closed, and the body is photographed that way, the face takes on an entirely different appearance that makes identification by wife or business partner almost impossible. Then, too, the lips are generally bloodless and of the same color as the victim's complexion. And the face, robbed of animation, seems more like a mask than something that had once been alive and warm. When a police photographer is taking a picture of a corpse for identification purposes, he must bring all the skills of a cosmetician to his work. Before lifting or relifting closed eyelids, he will insert glycerin and water into the sockets, to give the eyes a shine that will simulate in death the spark of life, and cause them to resemble false mirrors of the soul. He will daub the lips with dye and alcohol, restoring to them a blush which, if not quite kissable, is at least photographable. He will use powder and make-up, collodion or wax to achieve the desired result of having a photographed dead man look the way he might have when he was alive. (And nine times out of ten, when a person is shown such a photograph, he will immediately say, "He looks dead.")

Fingerprints and photographs do not identify a dead person. They only provide *means* of identification, assuming the unfortunate deceased had a police record or served in the armed forces or worked for municipal, state, or federal governments, or marched in anti-war protests; and/or further assuming that a friend or relative, when looking at a photograph, will jump up from his seat and shout, "Eureka, that's Harry!" It's nice when a corpse has a tattoo on the right biceps, a replica of the Golden Gate Bridge at sunset perhaps, with below it, in blue and red ink, the words "My name is Harry Lewis." Very few corpses are that obliging, though occasionally a tattoo will provide some insight into a dead man's past, or even his occupation. It is no secret, for example, that many tattooed men were, at one time in their lives, sailors. (But then again, if a man had been in the Navy, his fingerprints would be on file and there'd be no need for going the circuitous tattoo route.) Besides, there are even better ways of guessing at a dead man's occupation.

In many respects a dead and naked human being is no more easily identifiable than a slab of beef hanging in a butcher shop. The human being, however, *does* possess some physical characteristics that differentiate it from the beast of the field. Like hands and fingernails. A steer does not have hands and fingernails. Moreover, a steer does not use his hands and fingernails (which he doesn't have in the first place) to perform certain jobs linked with societal development. The human being does. A skilled medical examiner can therefore make some pretty shrewd occupational determinations based on the shape, length, condition, and trim of the fingernails as well as the calluses or lack of calluses on the fingers or other parts of the hand.

A workman's fingernails may be chipped, or caked with traces of his specialty—brick dust, plaster, soil, paint—and will rarely be manicured. A typist, pianist, court stenographer, or masseuse will definitely not have long fingernails. A man who repairs shoes will have a characteristic callus on his left thumb. An engraver will have a similarly identifiable callus on his right thumb. (Steers sometimes develop calluses on their hoofs, but these are caused by repeatedly pawing the ground and cannot be used as a means of establishing the occupation of the slaughtered animal.)

In truth, none of the M.E.'s career guesses serve as much more than guides to the detective in the field; if a pharmacist will characteristically have brittle fingernails, you can turn up a corpse with brittle fingernails who happens to be a pimp. Or a motion-picture producer. Or an airlines pilot. Or a ventriloquist. But a couple of guys with six corpses on their hands needed all the help they could get, and were grateful for whatever the lab or the medical examiner's office gave them.

Which in this case was nothing.

The six bodies in the ditch achieved a nice racial and ethnic balance. Three of them were black, two of them were Hispanic, and one of them was white. None of them carried any identifying scars or tattoos. None of them had hand or fingernail characteristics that could identify them as lacemakers or garage mechanics. None of them had any scrapings under their fingernails that proved decisive in linking them to an occupation. Worst of all, none of them had any fingerprint records. For all intents and purposes, they were all still as anonymous as the photographs taken of them, and the detectives still had no clue as to who had killed them or why.

STATEMENT of one Randall M. Nesbitt made this fourteenth day of January at 10:55 P.M. in the detective squadroom of the 87th Precinct on Grover Avenue in Isola. Randall Nesbitt freely and voluntarily offered the following information in the presence of Detective 2nd/Grade Stephen Louis Carella, Detective 3rd/Grade Bertram A. Kling, and attorney appointed for aforesaid Randall Nesbitt, Harold Finch of the law firm of Finch, Golden & Horowitz of 119 Cabot Street, Isola. Having been duly warned of his rights, and having waived his privilege to remain silent, Randall Nesbitt replied as follows to Detective Carella's question: *Why did you do it, Randy?*

Why? What do you mean "why"? I'm the president, that's why. I'm the elected leader, I can do what I want. I can order a hit when I want to, and if the orders ain't followed, there's trouble. I don't have to discuss the hit with nobody. I know what's best for my people, and I do what's best, and they listen to me, and they carry out the orders. The decisions I make ain't always popular, but I don't care about that, I'm not running no popularity contest. I'm doing what's best, and I'm the only one who can decide what's best because I'm the only one has all the facts at his fingertips. Those people were the enemy. I ordered the hit because I was trying to make peace.

Lots of guys in the clique, they think it's great to be president. An easy job, you know? But it ain't. It's a lonely job, and it's a job where the decisions you got to make ain't always understood right away. But I stand behind all the decisions I make, and I'm willing to take responsibility for them, even though I don't have to answer to nobody. I got my negotiator, and I got my war counselor, and they're two top men who I listen to, but even *they* know that what I say goes. I listen, I weigh the information, and then I decide. And it was me who decided to make the hit.

It was a complicated hit because there were two different cliques involved. The reason for the hit was to make peace between them and us. We'd been rapping since October, meetings down *our* clubhouse, meetings in *their* clubhouses, what did it accomplish? Nothing. You can talk only so long. After that, you got to make a show of strength. You got to show them who's the most powerful. Okay, I decided to show them. As it turned out, it didn't solve nothing because we later had to take even stricter measures. But I think it gave them reason to hesitate, you know? I think it made them look on us with respect. It made them say to themselves, "This guy is the president of the most powerful clique in the neighborhood. We better not fool around with him, because he's not kidding. He says he wants peace, and he means it." That's what the first hit must've made them think. After that, we had to get tougher.

There are guys in the clique who don't understand why I did what I did. They think it's easy. They didn't understand the first hit, and they still don't understand all the other things that happened. I'll tell you something. When you got these difficult decisions to make, and you finally make them, then you *expect* the people you're leading to *support* you, you know what I mean? I mean, man, these are your own *people,* you dig? They ain't supposed to raise objections, they ain't supposed to say this or that or the other thing. They're supposed to understand that I'm the president, and they're supposed to say, "Right on, man. Even if we don't like what you're doing, then maybe it's because we don't understand it yet. You go right ahead, man, you got our support." That's the way it's supposed to be. Instead, there were these cats on the inner council, they started complaining right away, the minute I told them the hit was already accomplished.

That was after Chingo reported back to me and told me he'd carried the bodies down to Isola, and dumped them in an open ditch on the North Side. So the council raised a stink. Like, man, who was *asking* them for their opinion? I almost ordered seven lashes. There's a club rule if you don't obey orders, you get seven lashes from each and every one of the members. Who was the council to question what I done? I swear, they're like children, you know what I mean? You got to take them by the hand and lead them every place, they wouldn't know how to wipe their own noses without me. Why am I the president? Why did they give me a mandate? To lead them, right? Okay, so I was leading them, and I wasn't about to take no back talk about how come I ordered a hit, and didn't I think it was going to just prolong matters, and maybe provoke other hits from the enemy against us, or bring down the fuzz, or whatever. I wasn't concerned with none of that. I was concerned with making peace.

Johnny, one of the guys on the council, got all upset about the baby.

Chingo told him that was an accident. When him

and Deucey and The Bullet busted in on the nigger and his chick, the kid was sleeping in a crib by the window, you know? So Chingo told them to take off all their clothes, the chick was half naked anyway, and then when the pair of them realized what was about to happen, the chick ran for the crib and scooped up the baby and was about to start yelling, you know? So that was when Chingo cut loose, not meaning to chop down the baby, but those things happen. You take action, you got to expect a few accidents. The baby was innocent, and nobody was trying to chop down an innocent baby. It just happened. Also, Chingo says that the nigger pulled a piece just as Chingo opened up, and maybe some stray bullets from his own gun killed the kid, who the hell knows? Like, you know, maybe *he* was responsible himself for killing his own baby. Like he saw Chingo with the piece in his hand, and he pulled his own piece to defend himself, and the bullets went wild. Chingo explained that to the council, and especially to Johnny, who was making all the noise. I finally kicked him out of the clubhouse, told him to go take a walk till he cooled off. We later had to deal with him on another matter, but that had nothing to do with his questioning the hit or the accident that happened during the hit.

The hit was complicated, like I said before. That's because there were two separate cliques to deal with. There was the Scarlet Avengers and the Death's Heads. We call them the *Heads* because half of them are junkies, though they won't admit it. We never call them heads to their faces, because the next thing you know you got another stabbing on your hands. You got to watch out for these jerks, they're so sensitive. Like when Jo-Jo got stabbed outside the junior high school on Yancey, because one of the Scarlets thought he was trying to make time with a Scarlet chick. Boy! Any of the guys in this clique even *looks* at one of them Scarlet dogs, that's the day I got to see. Anyway, that ain't the point. These guys get everything all mixed up. They're always looking for an excuse to say we done something, when most of the time we just mind our own business and try to do good. Who got rid of half the pushers in this neighborhood, if not us? Nobody ever thinks of that. They just go around saying things all the time, what do they know? I got a good clique here, we're a good clique. We try to set an example for all the others. And I'm the president, and I try always to do good, and that's the example I set for my own people.

I decided on the hit just after New Year's. Man, I spent nights pacing the floor thinking about it. I figured the only way to make them see reason was to grab them where it hurts, strike right in their own turf, get their leaders, show them we ain't afraid of nothing. I didn't talk it over with nobody. Not even Toy. I didn't even tell *her* nothing about it. I worked it out careful and then I told Doc, my negotiator, and Mace, my war counselor, and I listened to what they had to say about it, and they both said it was the right thing to do. It wouldn't have mattered what they said, because I already decided. But I showed them the respect of listening. A good leader's got to know when to listen in addition to when to act. The plan was to send Chingo and two raiders to get the president of the Scarlet Avengers and the president of the Heads. As it turned out, Chingo got more than we bargained for.

The baby, of course, was an accident, like I explained. But in addition, when Chingo and his raiders busted in on the *spic* pad, there was a blond cat sitting there rapping with the Head and his chick. He didn't know who the blond was at the time. We later found out in the newspapers. All Chingo saw was a white guy with a beard, maybe twenty-five, twenty-six years old, sitting there and rapping with the two spics. He was there to get the president. The chick was unfortunate. She shouldn't have been hanging around with a guy like that, who was holding up peace negotiations and putting himself in a vulnerable position. Those are the chances you take. The stranger was another matter. Chingo wasn't about to turn around and go out, now that he was there. Him and his raiders had already taken care of the other three, their bodies were downstairs in the back of the pickup truck, covered with a tarp. He was there to do the rest of the job, and so the stranger had to go with the other two. It was over in four seconds flat. If anybody in the building heard anything, they knew better than to open their mouths, or we'd have been around the next day to burn them out.

We don't fool around.

You're either our friends, or you're our enemies.

THE man on the telephone was a free-lance writer doing a magazine article on The Relationship of Television to Acts of Violence. That was not to be the title of his piece, he explained hastily. It was merely a statement of theme. The title would be something shorter and snappier. A title, he went on to explain, was almost as important as the first line of any written work, the hook that grabbed the reader at once and refused to let him go, no matter how he wiggled or squirmed.

The man's name was Montgomery Pierce-Hoyt.

Detective Meyer Meyer, normally a patient man, distrusted him at once, and listened to his long explanation of intent with boredom bordering on somnambulance. The first thing he distrusted was the man's name. Meyer Meyer did not know anybody who had a hyphenated family name. On his block, everyone had a very simple last name, no fancy hyphenation. Hyphenation was for companies like Colgate-Palmolive or Dow-Jones. Nor had he ever met a person with a first name like Montgomery. The only Montgomery he had ever heard of was Montgomery Ward, and that was another company. Who was he talking to here? A person or a company?

Meyer Meyer was very name-conscious because his own name had caused him no end of trouble and embarrassment. His father (bless his soul, his heart, and his sense of humor) had thought the double-barreled monicker would cause his offspring to stand out in a world of largely anonymous people, and (being something of a practical joker) had thought it funny besides (May he rest in peace; Meyer thought). Meyer had grown weary of telling people it was no fun to be raised as a Jew in a largely Gentile neighborhood, where his name inspired the chant "Meyer Meyer, Jew on fire" and on at least one occasion almost led to a backyard barbecue when it was thought necessary by various and assorted goyim to test the validity of the chant. Tying Meyer to a pole, they started a fire at his feet and then went off to their catechism class, where they were being taught devotion to Jesus, even though he might possibly have been a Jew. Meyer prayed, but nothing happened. Patiently, he prayed more fiercely and devoutly, and still nothing happened. It was beginning to get very hot down there near his sneakers. Patiently, never losing faith, he kept praying, and finally it began to rain, a veritable downpour that put out the flames at once. Oddly, Meyer did not become a religious man after his experience. Instead, he developed a deep sympathy for firemen and for hapless cavalry officers tied to the stake by savage Indians. He also developed an attitude of patience bordering on saintliness, which was perhaps a religious outcome, after all. His patience was wearing quite thin at the moment. Completely bald, burly, with china-blue eyes (the lids of which were dropping to half-mast) he listened to Montgomery Pierce-Hoyt on the telephone, and debated whether he should answer in cop talk.

"What I'm deeply interested in knowing," Pierce-Hoyt said, "is whether in your experience the acts of violence that confront you daily are in any way influenced or stimulated, consciously or unconsciously, by something the criminal may have seen on television."

"Mmm," Meyer said.

"What do you think?" Pierce-Hoyt said.

"*Who* did you say you were doing this story for?" Meyer asked.

"Nobody yet."

"Nobody yet," Meyer repeated, and nodded.

"But I'll sell it, don't worry," Pierce-Hoyt said. "So what do you think?"

"You want me to answer this on the telephone?" Meyer said. "Right this minute?"

"Well, yes, if . . ."

"Impossible," Meyer said.

"Why?"

"Because first of all, I have to check with the lieutenant. And second of all, how do I know you're really Mr. Pierce-Hoyt and not somebody else? And third of all, I have to gather my thoughts."

"Well, um, yes, I see," Pierce-Hoyt said. "Well, do you want me to come up there?"

"Not until I talk to the lieutenant and see if it's okay."

"When do you think you'll be able to talk to him?"

"Sometime today. Let me have your number and I'll get back to you in the morning."

"Fine," Pierce-Hoyt said, and gave Meyer the number. The other phone on Meyer's desk was ringing. He said an abrupt goodbye to Pierce-Hoyt and picked up the receiver.

"87th Squad, Detective Meyer," he said.

The caller was a woman who had seen the photographs of the multiple-murder victims in that morning's newspaper, and said she knew who the white man with the beard was.

THE woman's name was Phyllis Kingsley.

She lived in Isola, near the River Dix, which formed the southern boundary of the island. Had she lived two blocks farther uptown, she'd have been in that exclusive and luxurious section known as Stewart City. As it was, she lived in a tenement on a block with several furniture warehouses and two parking garages. Carella and Kling got there at eleven o'clock that Tuesday morning, January 8. The thermometer had risen only slightly; the temperature hovered in the mid-twenties. Phyllis Kingsley greeted them wrapped in a handwoven afghan, and told them something had been wrong with the heat all night long, and it still hadn't been fixed. They went into the living room, where the windows were covered with rime.

"We understand you can identify one of the murder victims," Carella said.

"Yes," Phyllis answered. She was a woman in her late thirties, with carrot-colored hair and green eyes that made her look very Irish. Her complexion was fair and sprinkled with freckles. She was not a pretty woman, and there was something about her manner that indicated vulnerability. The detectives waited, expecting her to say more than the single word "Yes." When it became apparent that nothing further was coming, Carella asked, "Who was he, can you tell us?"

"My brother," she said.

"His name?"

"Andrew Kingsley."

"How old was he?" Carella asked. He had exchanged a silent glance with Kling the moment the woman began talking. It was Kling, seated slightly to the left of her and beyond her field of vision, who now jotted the information into a notebook while Carella asked the questions, a technique that made the person talking feel more at ease.

"He was twenty-eight," Phyllis replied.

"Where did he live?" Carella asked.

"Here. Temporarily. He just arrived from California a few weeks ago."

"Did he have a job?"

"No. Well, on the Coast he had one. But he quit that to come here."

"What kind of work did he do?"

"I think he was a carhop. At one of the hamburger places they have out there."

"Why did he come to this city, Miss Kingsley, can you tell us?"

"Well, he said he'd been into a lot of things out there that helped him to find where his head was at, and he was anxious to get back East and put some of his ideas to work."

"What sort of ideas?"

"Well, he had ideas about the ghettos and of what he could do to help the people living in the ghettos. He was doing work in Watts out there."

"What kind of work?"

"He organized a drama group for the black kids in Watts. He was a drama major in college. That's why he went to California to begin with. He thought he could get work in the movies or in television, but you know . . ." She shrugged, and then clasped her hands in her lap.

"When did he arrive exactly, Miss Kingsley? From California, I mean. Would you remember?"

"It was two weeks ago yesterday."

"And he was living here? In this apartment?"

"Yes. I have an extra room."

"Did he know anybody in this city? Besides you?"

"He was born and raised here. He knew a lot of people."

"The other pictures in the paper . . ."

"No," she said, and shook her head.

"You didn't recognize any of them?"

"No."

"You wouldn't know whether any of them were your brother's friends."

"None of them looked familiar."

"Did he *have* black friends? Or Puerto Ricans?"

"Yes."

"Did you ever meet any of them?"

"No."

"Did you ever meet *any* of his friends?"

"Yes, he brought a man home with him one night."

"A white man?"

"Yes."

"Would you remember his name?"

"David Harris."

"Did your brother introduce him as one of his friends?"

"They had just met, I believe."

"Do you know what kind of work he did?"

"He didn't say. I got the feeling . . ." She shook her head.

"Yes, go on."

"I didn't like him very much."

"Why not?"

"I don't know. He seemed . . . I felt he was not a good person."

"What made you feel that, Miss Kingsley?"

"He seemed . . . violent. I had the feeling he was capable of enormous violence. He made me extremely uncomfortable. I'm glad Andy never brought him back here again."

"How old was he?"

"In his thirties, I would guess."

"Any idea where he lives?"

"In the Quarter, I think. He mentioned Audibon Avenue. That's in the Quarter, isn't it?"

"Yes. What else can you tell us about him?"

"Do you think he killed my brother?"

"We have no ideas about that as yet, Miss Kingsley."

"I'll bet he did," Phyllis said, and nodded gently. "He seemed like the kind of person who could do murder."

"What did he look like?"

"He was very tall and quite good-looking. A dark complexion, longish brown hair."

"When was he here with your brother?"

"A week ago? Six days ago? I'm not sure."

"When did you last see your brother alive?"

"Sunday night."

"Did he say where he was going?"

"He said he had business uptown."

"*Where* uptown?"

"He only said uptown."

"What kind of business?"

"He didn't say."

"What time did he leave here?"

"About six o'clock."

"Did he say what time he'd be back?"

"No."

"Were you expecting him back?"

"I had no expectations either way. He often stayed out all night. He had his own key. He was an adult, I never questioned him about his comings and goings."

"What was he wearing the last time you saw him?"

"A Navy pea jacket, a plaid shirt, dark trousers . . . brown or blue, I'm not sure."

"Hat? Gloves?"

"Black leather gloves, no hat."

"Muffler?"

"No."

"Wallet? Keys?"

"He had a black leather wallet, I assume he was carrying it with him. The only key he had was the key to this apartment."

"We're very anxious to know where he might have been heading on the night he was killed, Miss Kingsley. Would your brother have kept a diary, or an appointment book, or even a calendar on which he might have marked . . . ?"

"I'll show you his room," Phyllis said, and rose, and pulled the afghan tighter around her shoulders, and led them through the apartment. There were four rooms altogether: the living room in which they had interrogated Phyllis, a kitchen, and two bedrooms. Andrew Kingsley's room was at the end of a long windowless corridor. The corridor was hung with photographs of people dressed in clothing of the thirties, forties, and fifties. Carella assumed they were family pictures. The pictures could have been taken anywhere in the city. Or anywhere in *any* city, for that matter. There was one picture of a very young boy standing before what looked like a late-forties automobile. Carella hesitated before it, and Phyllis immediately said, "My brother. He was only four when the picture was taken." In the next breath she said, "It's hard to believe he's dead. He's been gone from this city for a long time, first to college and then California, it's not that I saw him that often. And yet . . . it's hard to believe. It's very hard to believe."

"Are your parents alive, Miss Kingsley?" Carella asked.

"No. They were killed in an automobile accident in France, seven years ago. It was the first time they'd been to Europe. My mother had wanted to go all her life, and they'd finally saved enough money." She shook her head and fell silent.

"Do you have any other brothers or sisters?"

"No. I'm alone now," she said.

Andrew Kingsley's room contained a dresser and a bed. There were very few articles of clothing in the dresser, and even fewer in the closet. There were no diaries, notebooks, appointment books, or calendars. A package of cheap stationery was in the top drawer of his dresser. One sheet of paper had been pulled from the others and a letter had been started. The beginning of the unfinished letter read:

Dear Lisa,

How are you, golden girl? I am enjoying every minute of being here. The only sad part is that you're not with me, and I hope you've been giving some serious

"Is this your brother's handwriting?" Carella asked.

"Let me see," Phyllis said, and looked at the page he extended. "Yes."

"Any idea who Lisa might be?"

"No."

"Are these all his personal belongings?"

"Yes. He . . . didn't have very much."

"Miss Kingsley," Carella said, "I don't wish to compound your grief, but if you could find it in yourself to go over to the hospital and identify your brother . . ."

"Yes, but . . . do I have to do it today? I'm not feeling too well. That's why I'm home from work."

"What kind of work do you do?"

"I'm a bookkeeper. I felt something coming on last night, and I took some cold pills, and I'd probably have been all right if the heat hadn't gone on the fritz. I felt absolutely awful this morning. In fact, I was still in bed when my neighbor came in to show me the newspaper. And my brother's picture."

"You can go over there tomorrow, if you like. If you're feeling better," Carella said.

"Yes. Which hospital is it?"

"Buena Vista. On Culver Avenue."

"Yes, all right," she said. "Was there anything else?"

"No. Thank you, Miss Kingsley, you've been very helpful."

As she led them to the front door, she said, "He was a good boy. He hadn't found himself yet, but he was trying. I loved him a lot. I'm going to miss him. It's not that I saw him that often . . ."

She began weeping then.

She fumbled with the door lock, managed at last to twist it open, and then covered her nose and her mouth with one hand, the tears spilling from her eyes, and let them out of the apartment, and locked the door behind them. As they went down the steps they could hear her still weeping behind the locked door of the apartment in which she lived alone again.

THE Isola telephone directory listed one David Harris on South Philby, and another on Avenue Y in the Quarter. A look at a street map of the city showed that Avenue Y crossed Audibon at one point, and they assumed that this was the address they wanted. They hit the apartment at close to noon. They knocked five times in succession before they got an answer, and then the voice was muffled, as though it were coming from someplace deep inside the apartment. They knocked again.

"Okay, okay," a voice shouted.

They heard footsteps approaching the door.

"Who is it?" the voice asked.

"Police," Kling said. "Want to open up, please?"

They were totally unprepared for what happened next.

If they considered Harris a possible suspect, it was only because Phyllis had described him as a violent person. Other than that, they had no reason to believe that he had killed six people. They were here to ask questions about the extent of his relationship with Kingsley. They were here, too, because Harris was the only link to the life Andrew Kingsley was living outside his sister's apartment. They wanted to know what, if anything, Harris could tell them about that life, in the hope that the information would shed some light on how or why Kingsley had ended up dead in a ditch with five other people. Their intentions were peaceful.

They changed their minds in the next ten seconds.

In the next ten seconds, or eight seconds, or six seconds, or however long it took the person behind the door to squeeze the trigger of a gun three times in rapid succession, they changed their minds about peaceful intentions, suspects, and laws that prohibited the kicking-in of doors. The explosions were shockingly loud, the wood paneling on the door shattered, the bullets struck the plaster wall opposite and began ricocheting wildly in the narrow corridor. Kling and Carella were already on the floor. Carella's pistol was in his hand, and Kling's was coming out of its holster. Three more shots splintered the wooden door, buzzed overhead, whistled in ricochet.

"That's six," Carella said.

He scrambled to one side of the door and got to his feet. Kling, following his suit, crawled to the other side of the door and stood up. They looked across the door at each other, and hesitated, only because the decision they made in the next several seconds could cost either one of them his life. Six shots had been fired. Had the man inside exhausted the ammunition in a six-shot revolver, and was he now reloading? Or was he armed with an automatic, some of which had a capacity of eleven cartridges? Carella heard his watch ticking. If he waited any longer, the man would have reloaded even if he were toting a revolver. He made his move instantly, and Kling picked up on it like a quarterback following his blocker. Carella moved swiftly to the wall opposite the door, put his back against it for support and leverage, lifted his knee like a piston, and kicked out flat-footed at the lock. The lock sprang on the first kick, and Carella rushed forward at once, following the door as it opened into the room, Kling peeling off immediately behind him as he passed the doorjamb.

A huge and hugely handsome man was inserting a cartridge into the cylinder of what looked like a Colt

.38. He was standing about five feet from the door, and he was wearing only pajama bottoms, and the moment Carella and Kling burst into the room, he dropped the cartridges he was holding in the palm of his left hand and swung the gun hand into position. Carella, because he had learned over the years that yelling had more effect than whispering, shouted "Drop it!" and right behind him Kling yelled "Drop the gun!" and the man, who they assumed was Harris, hesitated a moment, and looked from one to the other of them, and made his own decision in the nick of time because each of the cops would have given him only another second before they shot him down where he stood. He dropped the gun. It clattered to the floor. He was wearing only pajama bottoms, but they threw him up against the wall anyway, and tossed him, and then slapped him into handcuffs.

They were both breathing very hard.

3

DON'T read nothing.

I don't have to read nothing. The clique has been mentioned a couple of times in the papers, and there's always reporters up here nosing around. But I don't talk to reporters, and I don't read what they write. That way I can keep cool. Whenever we have a meeting, I'm the coolest man in the room. That's because my head ain't cluttered. I hardly ever go to the flicks or watch television, either, except for football. I like football. I like to figure out the plays. It's like figuring out life, you know what I mean? Those guys down there on the field are thinking every minute, and they're alert to danger, and they react automatically. Before I graduated from Whitman, which is the high school over on Crestview, I was on the football team. That's the only decent thing I ever got out of that school, being on the team. I wasn't the quarterback or nothing, I was just in the line. I'm a big guy, you know, and I was even huskier then, when I was a kid. That always stuck with me, my experience on the football team. Watching the games on television relaxes me and helps me make decisions. Reading only gets me confused. A person has got to keep a clear head all the time.

Anyway, it was Mace who brung the newspaper to me on Wednesday and read about the guy the fuzz had picked up, and how he was maybe linked some way to the bearded guy Chingo and the raiders had shot. The newspaper story told who the dead guy was, some cat named Andrew Kingsley, who had just come in from California a little while ago. He should have stood where he was. It didn't say what he'd been doing in that spic pad, and it also didn't say who the spics were. That figured. If I knew anything about the Death's Heads (man, that name really kills me!), it was that they weren't about to run to the fuzz and identify none of their people. Around here, the fuzz are trouble, no matter which end of the stick you're holding. You call them in because somebody busted your legs with a baseball bat, and next thing you know, *you're* the one being sent to jail for bleeding on the sidewalk. The

Heads knew better than to tell the cops it was their president who got shot and dumped in the ditch. The cops would have to find that out for themselves, and according to the story Mace read me from the newspaper, they weren't doing such a hot job of it. And the Scarlets wouldn't tell the cops nothing neither. If they did anything at all, it would be they'd try to settle the score. Which is why we were being very careful those first few days after the hit.

We got a very tight security system around here, anyway. We don't let nobody near us. We got sentries posted on all the rooftops and on all the street corners. There ain't nobody who can come anywhere close to the clubhouse without us knowing it way in advance. Even before Mace knocked on the door and brought me the newspaper, I knew he was on the way. I don't trust nobody, not even Mace. All the members got orders that whoever's approaching the clubhouse, even if it's another member, the president's got to know about it. Four minutes before Mace knocked on the door, a runner came and told me he was on the way up. That's the way I like it.

The clubhouse is on the third floor of this abandoned building on 57th. We got it painted in these nice Day-Glo colors in a sort of abstract design, you know? The Bullet, aside from being an experienced combat trooper, is also quite an artist. He designed the pictures on the walls, and he painted them with the help of some of the younger kids in the clique. We don't have no obscene pictures on our walls, like some of the other cliques have. No pictures of naked women, nothing like that. I don't go for that kind of stuff, and I made it clear to the members that I won't tolerate nothing like that around the clubhouse. Sex is a private thing you do in private with the person you love. I don't go for dirty actions, and I don't go for dirty talk, either. One of our rules is no profanity. You hear me say a dirty word in all the time I've been talking to you? You bet you didn't. I pride myself on that. Oh, sure, I know it's easier to express yourself in language that's not correct. But I've never been a person who took the easy road. I don't go *looking* to do things the hard way, but I guess it's my nature to make sure things come out *right,* you know? And that goes for language, too. And that's why I never swear, I never even say "hell" or "damn," I'm just saying them now as an example. And I don't allow none of the people around me to use profanity neither. Sure, I could be permissive about it, let the guys say whatever they want to, let them bring in the chicks and ball them right in the clubhouse, let them smoke pot, all of that. But I don't believe in it. It's not right, none of them things are right.

I know there's been commissions formed and they gave reports on hash, and they say it don't hurt to smoke it, and it ain't habit-forming, and all that. I don't care *what* the commissions say. As long as I'm president, I'll listen to my own heart and my own head on what's right and what's wrong. And you can't tell me that these movies they're showing, and these magazines that are on the stands, and these dirty books these guys are writing are right. 'Cause they ain't.

They're wrong. The way cursing is wrong. When I was on Whitman's football team, anytime the coach heard anybody say a dirty word, it was eight laps around the field. You ever run eight laps around a football field? You learn not to curse pretty quick.

Mace said the cops—was it you guys?—had picked up a hood named David Harris, who opened fire on them the minute they knocked on the door. He was described as an unemployed laborer with a police record for assault and burglary. What he admitted, after the cops questioned him, was that he had held up a liquor store in Calm's Point the night before, and when they knocked on the door and said it was the police, he figured they were coming to bust him for the armed robbery. Which led them to questioning him about his relationship with this Andrew Kingsley cat, who Chingo and the boys had knocked off together with the Head spic and his girl. Harris said he hardly knew Kingsley from a hole in the wall. He had met him in a bar a week or so ago, and they had got to talking about life on the Coast, where Harris had spent some time—probably in jail—and then Kingsley had asked him up to meet his sister, and that was that. Harris said he didn't get along too hot with Kingsley's sister, who he described as a "very up-tight lady." He also said it came as news to him that Kingsley had been found dead in a ditch on the North Side, since Harris (like me) don't read newspapers. It looked good. The cops still didn't know who any of the other people in the ditch were, and they weren't about to find out, either.

But then Midge opened her mouth.

THE telephone on Carella's desk rang at two-fifteen on Wednesday afternoon, January 9, the day after they had busted David Harris and charged him with Armed Robbery. The story of his arrest had run in both morning newspapers, and had made headlines in the afternoon tabloid. The pictures of the six unknown victims were still running in all three papers, and Carella was still hoping, but not expecting, that someone would come forward to identify them. Identification of Andrew Kingsley, rather than simplifying matters, had complicated them for Carella and Kling—who until then had suspected the ditch murders were related to organized crime. (You have to start someplace, and organized crime is as good a place as any to leap off from when you find six bodies piled up in an open trench.) Their assumption hadn't been altogether unreasonable; the police all over the city had recently been plagued by an outbreak of shootings, the result of a struggle between old-line white racketeers and upstart blacks and Puerto Ricans.

The cause of this struggle was quite simple. The white hoods had held absolute control over the lucrative narcotics trade for a very long time now, and whereas they did not mind *selling* dope to blacks and Puerto Ricans, they did not appreciate blacks and Puerto Ricans muscling into their brisk little industry and trying to corner some of the profits for themselves. There is one sure way to discourage free enterprise, and that is to put a bullet in your competitor's nostril. Unidentified bodies kept turning up in deserted alleys or outdoor parking lots or in the trunks of abandoned Plymouths of unknown vintage. And since the underworld (white *or* black) stringently observed the code of *omerta,* roughly translated from the Italian as "Mum's the word, sweetheart," there was rarely anyone brave or stupid enough to step forward and identify an unknown corpse. The possibility had therefore existed that the six bodies in the ditch were related to the racial narcotics war. But that didn't explain the presence of the bearded white man, Andrew Kingsley, who had no record at all, and who—according to his sister—had been engaged in only noble pursuits on the West Coast. As it turned out, the cops had been thinking correctly in terms of gang warfare, but they were thinking a little big. The call from the girl named Midge caused them to lower their sights a bit.

"Steve, this is Dave Murchison on the desk downstairs."

"Yeah, Dave?" Carella said.

"I got a girl on the line, says she wants to talk to whoever's handling the ditch murders. I guess that's you.

"Put her on," Carella said, and moved a pad into place near the telephone.

"Hello?" a girl's voice said. She was either whispering or she had a bad cold, Carella couldn't tell which.

"This is Detective Carella," he said. "Can I help you, miss?"

"Detective who?" she whispered.

"Carella. Who's speaking, please?"

"Midge."

"What's your last name, Midge?"

"Never mind," the girl said. "I have to make this fast. I'm alone right now, but they'll be back. If they catch me calling you . . ."

"*Who* are you talking about, Midge?"

"The ones who killed those people in the ditch. I didn't know there was a baby involved. The minute Johnny told me there was a baby involved . . ."

"Johnny who?"

"Never mind. He told me about it even before I seen the pictures in the paper. I told him I was gonna call up and say who done it. He said they would break my arms and legs."

"*Who, Midge?*"

"The black man in the ditch was Lewis Atkins, he was president of a club called the Scarlet Avengers. The girl was his wife . . . Are you listening?"

"I'm listening, Midge," Carella said.

"It was their baby got killed. That wasn't right. I told Johnny it wasn't right, and he said he'd take it up with the council."

"What's Johnny's last name?"

"I don't want him to get in trouble," the girl said. "He got in trouble once before when he stood up for me. I don't want that to happen again."

"Who were the other people in the ditch? Can you tell me that?"

"The Spanish guy was president of the Death's

44

Heads. His real name is Eduardo Portoles, but he signs himself Edward the First. The girl, I'm not sure. I think her name was Constantina, but I'm not sure."

"Who killed them, Midge?"

There was no answer.

"Midge, where are you calling from?"

There was still no answer. Carella realized all at once that the line was dead. He had not heard the click of a receiver being replaced on its cradle. Someone had either cut the wire or yanked the phone from the wall.

WE had trouble with Johnny and his chick before, so this was nothing new. Only this time it was a little more serious.

The first trouble with them was when Midge got pregnant and wanted to have an abortion. I know abortions are legal in this state, but to me that's murder. Midge belonged to our women's auxiliary, and that made her a member of the clique, and that meant she abided by the rules, and the rules say no killing except in self-defense. I want to make that clear. All the stuff that happened with the Scarlets and the Heads, and all the stuff that happened later, was in self-defense. It was done for the general good of the members. To protect the clique. What we done to Midge was also done to protect the clique. We went easy on her because she's a girl.

The first static was about the abortion, back in April of last year, long before I was re-elected. I got nothing to say about what goes on personally between the members and their chicks, so long as there's no public display in the clubhouse. Okay, Johnny should've been more careful, but he wasn't. So Midge got pregnant and she come to me and said she was thinking of going down the clinic and having an abortion. I got to explain this girl Midge. First of all, she's got a big mouth. Not only big, but loud. And she's always on the telephone. I thought *I* was the world's telephone champ, but Midge has me beat solid when it comes to talking. Anyway, I don't use the phone for common gossip. I'll call somebody to congratulate them, like one of the guys in the clique who done a good job, I'll call to tell him how I appreciate it. Or, like, I used to call the radio stations. This was a couple of months ago, before one of the stations sent a reporter up here to talk to guys on all the clubs, and he talked to every one of the clubs but *us*. So naturally they bad-mouthed us, when they didn't know a thing about how we operate or what we're trying to do. I don't call the radio stations no more, but I used to call disc jockeys, you know, and tell them I was president of a club up in Riverhead, and we were listening to his show right that minute and thought he was doing a great job, and would he play this or that song for us? It was friendly, you know? Now I got nothing to do with those radio guys, not since they started saying bad things about us. And, I'll tell you, they better watch out what they say in the future. I mean, if this thing gets in the papers—you think it'll get in the papers?—they better watch what they say. We got plenty of members. Plenty.

But Midge used to get on that phone just for gossip. Like something would happen, we'd do something, and right away she was on the hot line spreading it to the other girls in the clique. She was a big mouth, plain and simple. And she was always hugging everybody, throwing her arms around them the minute they came through the door, and calling everybody "Sweetheart," or "Honey," or "Darling." It was disgusting. I never liked that chick. I put up with her only because I thought Johnny was a valuable man. We should have been stricter with her, and maybe we should've taken care of him at the same time. Saved ourselves a lot of headaches later on. But nobody's perfect. I try to handle things as they come up, and they don't always come up according to the game plan. That's the time to weave and dodge and figure things out on your feet. That's the time it pays to be the coolest man around, no panic.

I told her, last April, no abortion. She wanted to know what she was supposed to do. She was only fifteen years old, she didn't want no kid, and Johnny's mother wouldn't let them get married. I told her put the kid up for adoption. I also told her she better go buy some pills or a diaphragm or a coil or whatever (which wasn't talking dirty, I was talking to her like a doctor or a priest) and avoid that kind of accident in the future. She had the baby in November, and the adoption people took it away without her ever seeing it. She didn't even know whether it was a boy or a girl. Big mouth, of course, went all over the neighborhood saying I had stolen her baby from her. I almost rapped her in the mouth when word got back to me. Johnny told me to please forgive her because she was a very excitable type and them taking the baby away from her like that was very emotionally upsetting. I told Johnny it was *her* who wanted to kill the baby in the first place, so what was she yelling about now? Johnny said he would talk to her and calm her down. But, man, when you got a big mouth like Midge, there's nothing you can do with her except take care of her.

Which is what we done when we found her on the telephone.

It was Johnny, you know, who raised all the fuss in the council when he found out Chingo had accidentally killed the baby. It later turned out that Johnny was only saying what Midge *told* him to say. Like, you know, there was a whole psychological thing going on there, and it traced right back to her having put up her own baby for adoption. Don't ask me about it because I don't understand none of this psychological stuff too good. There was one time when I got in trouble, I was forced to go see a shrink because I was on probation, you know? Man, I didn't learn *nothing* from that guy. Later on, when I was first nominated for president of the clique, somebody raised the idea—like a smear tactic, right?—that I had been seeing this shrink, and maybe I wasn't qualified to be president, and all that. Like a president is supposed to make quick, cool decisions and not be unbalanced, and this guy who raised the idea (I forget his name, he moved to Chicago with his mother) said like maybe I was crazy because I had been seeing this shrink to satisfy my probation officer. I won the election anyway. And I got *re*-elected, too.

But what I'm saying is that Midge got all mixed up in her head about the baby Chingo had accidentally killed, and the baby the adoption agency had taken away from her in November, and she started nagging Johnny to raise it in the council—not that I know what he expected to accomplish. The baby was already dead, no? And then, when he went back to her and told her I'd put him down, told him to take a walk and cool off, well, the thing kept stewing inside her until finally she decided to call the cops. Two of the guys were up this other chick's house—Ellie, her name is. They felt like having some pizza, so Ellie and the two of them went downstairs to get it, and they left Midge alone with the telephone. She can't resist a telephone. She sees one sitting there, man, she gets the itch to pick it up and dial it, and start shooting off her big mouth. So the minute she was alone she called the cops and was reeling off the names of the people in the ditch when The Bullet come back in because he forgot his cigarettes, and he heard what she was doing, and he pulled the phone out of the wall.

We made her stand before the inner council. It was tough on Johnny, because this was his chick, and she done something real wrong, and he was one of the guys who had to decide what the punishment would be. We could've done whatever we wanted with her. Her mother is dead, you know, and her father's a wino who raped her when she was eleven, and who she was scared to even be in the same building with. Most of the time she slept in the clubhouse, even though the only heat there is from these kerosene burners we put around. It's an abandoned building, did I tell you that? I guess I told you that. So we could've done whatever we wanted, there was nobody to know, and nobody to care—except maybe Johnny. We could've had her killed. She was threatening the security.

The council voted to cut out her tongue.

Johnny asked for clemency, and I granted it. The council didn't like my veto, but if the council's wrong, I don't care *how* they vote. Around Christmas time they voted that the money in our treasury should be turned over to this neighborhood group that was trying to fix up one of the empty lots as a park. Paint the walls of the buildings around it, you know, and put in benches and maybe even plant some grass. There was two hundred and sixty dollars in the treasury, and I couldn't see wasting it on an empty lot when we still needed more guns and ammunition for the clique's defense. So I said no. I'm the president, and I got the power of veto. But the council overroded my veto, and voted the money again, so you know what I did? I told Big Anthony, who's the treasurer and who's in charge of the clique's bankbook, to go to the bank and take out the money, just leaving a couple of bucks in it to keep the account active. And he brung me two hundred and fifty-five dollars, and I impounded the funds. I still got the money. It's in a safe place and I won't touch a dime of it, because it belongs to the clique. But I ain't turning it over to those neighborhood do-gooders, neither, no matter *what* the council voted.

Why I vetoed their wanting to cut out Midge's tongue had nothing to do with Johnny's pitch for clemency. What I figured was that she already done the damage, she already talked to the cops. Which meant that they'd be coming around looking for her, trying to get the rest of the story from her. So either we had to kill her to shut her up completely, or we had to get her out of sight. In matters of security, I usually show no mercy, I mean it. And this was a matter of security, no question about it. But I guess I was feeling generous that day. I could've said "Get rid of her," and Chingo or The Bullet would've dumped her in the river without batting an eyelash. But instead, there's this place that Big Anthony's aunt has in the next state, just over the Hamilton Bridge, and she goes there in the summertime, she grows corn there, it's a nice little place. In the winter, though, it's closed up, but Big Anthony has a key and we sometimes go out there with the chicks and make a fire and sit around. I told Big Anthony to pick another member, anyone he wanted, and take Midge out there and keep her there for a week or so, till things cooled down. I also told him twenty lashes on her back every morning and every night, and she better not scream. If she screamed—and Midge was standing there through all this—I wanted to know about it, and then I'd forget how decent I was being and I'd tell the council to go ahead and do to her what they wanted.

She got the message. Or at least it looked that way. But even in spite of what we were forced to do later, I think I done the correct thing at the time. I could just as easy have lost my cool and told the council to go ahead, do what they wanted. But I didn't. Which is why I'm the leader, and they're the council. When you're the leader, you got to know when to use the power you got, and when not to. You got to be absolutely hard sometimes, and sometimes you got to be moderate. It's a balance you achieve, you know what I mean? When I got re-elected I made a little speech up the clubhouse. I told the members I wanted them to pray that I'd have God's help in making decisions that were right for them.

I myself pray to God every night that I'll always do the right thing. And I think my people must pray for me, too, like I asked them to. Because I *did* do the right thing about Midge, even though I never could stand her, and even though later on, it might have looked like the wrong decision.

4

THERE were five sections to the city, and Riverhead was one of them. It was separated from Isola by the Diamondback River, which flowed from the River Harb, snaked southward and then westward, and then emptied into the River Dix on the southern side of the island. There were no rivers in Riverhead itself. There were several reservoirs, and two lakes, and a brook called Five Mile Pond. The brook was not five miles long, nor was it five miles wide, nor was it five miles from any significant landmark. The origin and evolution of the name were obscure. It was probably called Five Mile Pond for much the same reason that Riverhead, which did not have a river in it, was called Riverhead.

Once upon a time, when the world was young and the Dutch were snugly settled in the city, the land adjacent to Isola was owned by a patroon named Pieter Ryerhert. Ryerhert was a farmer who at the age of sixty-eight grew tired of rising with the chickens and going to bed with the cows. As the metropolis grew, and the need for housing beyond Isola's limited boundaries increased, Ryerhert sold or donated most of his land to the expanding city, and then moved down to Isola, where he lived the gay life of a fat, rich burgher. Ryerhert's Farms became simply Ryerhert, but this was not a particularly easy name to pronounce. By the time World War I rolled around, and despite the fact that Ryerhert was Dutch and not German, the name really began to rankle, and petitions were circulated to change it because it sounded too Teutonic, and therefore probably had Huns running around up there cutting off the hands of Belgian babies. It became Riverhead in 1919. It was still Riverhead—but not the Riverhead it had been then.

Except for the easternmost part, where Carella still lived, most of the area had begun deteriorating in the early 1940's, and had continued its downward plunge unabated over the years. It was, in fact, difficult to believe that West Riverhead was actually a part of the biggest city in the richest country in the world—but there it was, folks, just a brisk short walk over the

Thomas Avenue Bridge. Half a million people lived on the other side of that bridge in a jagged landscape as barren as the moon's. Forty-two percent of those people were on the city's welfare rolls, and of those who were capable of holding jobs, only twenty-eight percent were actually employed. Six thousand abandoned buildings, heatless and without electricity, lined the garbage-strewn streets. An estimated 17,000 drug addicts found shelter in those buildings when they were not marauding the streets in competition with packs of vicious dogs. The statistics for West Riverhead were overwhelming; their weight alone would have seemed enough to have reduced that section of the city to rubble—26,347 new cases of tuberculosis reported each year; 3,412 cases of malnutrition; 6,502 cases of venereal disease. For every hundred babies born in West Riverhead, three died while still in infancy. For those who survived, there was a life ahead of grinding poverty, helpless anger, and hopeless frustration. It was no wonder that the police there had dossiers on more than 9,000 street-gang members. It was these dossiers that caused Carella and Kling to cross the Thomas Avenue Bridge on Thursday morning, January 10.

They had spoken to a detective named Charles Broughan of Riverhead's 101st, who immediately recognized the names of the gangs Midge had given Carella on the telephone, and told them to come right on up. They were, of course, familiar with West Riverhead because as working cops their investigations almost always took them beyond the boundaries of their own precinct. But neither of the two men had been up there for several months now, and were somewhat shocked by the rapid rate of disintegration. Even the front of the decrepit brick building next door to the 101st had been spray-painted with graffiti, a seeming impossibility for a street where cops constantly came and went, day and night. Sly 46, Terror 17, Ape 11, Louis III, Angel Marker 24, Absolute I, Shaft 18—on and on, the pseudonyms trailed their curlicues and loops, and dotted their i's, and crossed their t's, in reds and yellows and blues and purples, overlapping, obliterating the brick and each other to create a design as complex as any Jackson Pollock painting.

Carella could not understand the motivation. Presumably, this was a new form of pop art, in which the signature of the painter became the painting itself, the medium became the message. But assuming the message was a bid for recognition in a city that imposed anonymity, then why didn't the artist sign his own name, rather than the nickname by which he was known only to his immediate friends? (One of the names sprayed in yellow paint was indeed Nick 42, a *real* "Nick" name, Carella thought, and winced.) Of course, spraying the sides of buildings with virtually impossible-to-remove paint was not exactly a legal enterprise, so perhaps the sprayers were using *aliases* rather than *pseudonyms,* a subtle distinction recognized only by serious poets writing pornography on the side. Carella shrugged and followed Kling into the precinct.

Most of the older precincts in the city resembled each other the way distant cousins do. The detectives identified themselves at the familiar high wooden muster desk, with its polished brass railing bolted to the floor and its sign advising all visitors to inquire at the desk, and then followed a hand-lettered sign that read DETECTIVE DIVISION, up the iron-runged steps, past chipped and peeling walls painted apple-green back during the Spanish-American War when the nation was young and crime was on the decrease, and then down a narrow corridor in which there were frosted-glass doors lettered in black—INTERROGATION ROOM, CLERICAL, LOCKER ROOM, MEN'S ROOM, LADIES' ROOM—and came up against a slatted wooden railing that divided the corridor from the Detective Squadroom of the One-Oh-One. It was like coming home.

Charlie Broughan was a big beefy cop with a two days' growth of beard on his face. He explained that he'd been working a homicide ("I'm *always* working a goddamn homicide up here") and hadn't had time to sleep, much less shave. He went immediately to his files on the precinct's street gangs, dug out a stack of manila folders, dumped them on the desk, and said, "Here's the stuff. We've got 'em filed by gang names, names of members, and also geographical locations, all cross-indexed. That stuff represents two years' work, I want you to know. Those little bastards out there think we got nothing to do but keep track of their comings and goings. You're welcome to look at them, but don't get 'em out of order, okay, because the lieutenant'll string me up in the backyard if you do. When you're finished, just give 'em to Danny Finch in the Clerical Office, and he'll see they get back where they belong. I'd stay with you, but I got to go downtown and check a hotel register where we think we got a lead on this son of a bitch who's been picking up hookers and checking into hotels with them, and then stabbing them while he's humping them—nice guy, huh? We sent out a sample signature, a phony name he signed in the register on the job he did next-to-last, up here in a fleabag on Yates. This guy downtown near the tunnel, night clerk at a hotel there, thinks he recognizes the handwriting from a guy who checked in two nights ago. Guy's gone now, and he used a different name, of course, but maybe we can get somebody to tell us what the hell he even *looks* like. *If* the handwriting matches, which it probably won't. Only good thing about this, if it turns out he is the guy, is that this time he couldn't get no broad up there in the room with him to cut up. What a fuckin' city, I'm telling you, I'm thinking of moving to Tokyo or some other place quiet. I'll see you," he said, and waved, and took his name off the duty roster and put on his coat and hat and went shambling off down the corridor like a giant disgruntled bear.

They sat at his desk, and began going through the manila folders.

EVEN when Carella and Kling were still two blocks away from the clubhouse of the Death's Heads, they began seeing the signature of the gang's president scrawled in paint on the walls of apartment buildings. "He signs himself Edward the First," Midge had said, and "Edward I" was as visible in this six-block section of West Riverhead as were pictures of Mao Tse-tung in China. The area itself was a bewildering mixture of white, black, and Puerto Rican camps, each vaguely defined enclave bordering on the other and spilling over dangerously into disputed no-man's lands. Eduardo Portoles had lived (according to the 101st's dossier) two blocks from the clubhouse, at 1103 Concord Avenue, between a Puerto Rican *bodega* and a shop selling dream books and herbs and numerology guides, and the like. There were, of course, no names in the broken lobby mailboxes, but the 101st's records had indicated that Portoles lived on the top floor of the building, in Apartment 43.

This time Carella and Kling stood on either side of the doorjamb as Carella leaned over to knock. They had not drawn their guns, but their overcoats were open and their holsters were within easy reach. They need not have worried. The person who opened the door was a little girl who stared up at them out of wide brown eyes.

"Hello," Carella said.

The little girl did not answer. She was perhaps five years old, certainly no older than six. She was wearing a cotton petticoat, and she was barefoot, and she sucked at her thumb and said nothing, the brown eyes peering up at them unflinchingly.

"What's your name?" Carella asked.

The girl did not answer.

"You think she understands?" Kling said.

"I doubt it. *Hablas tú español?*" Carella said.

The girl nodded.

"Está alguien contigo aquí?"

The girl shook her head.

"Estás sola?"

"*Sí,*" she said, and nodded. *"Sí, estoy sola."*

"Quién vive aquí contigo?"

"Eduardo y Constantina."

"What'd she say?" Kling asked.

"She said she lives here with Eduardo and Constantina. But she's alone now, there's no one with her. I wonder if she knows they're dead."

"Let's check inside," Kling said.

"Perdóname," Carella said to the little girl, *"nosotros queremos entrar."*

The girl stepped aside. As they went into the apartment Carella said, *"Cómo te llamas?"* and the girl answered, *"Maria Lucia."*

There were pots and pans piled in the sink, and dirty dishes on the kitchen table. In the living room, the television set was on, but the volume control was apparently broken, and animated cartoon figures pranced across the screen in a chase without words or music. On the bedroom floor, strewn about in confusion and haste, the detectives found clothing belonging to a man and a woman. A large quantity of blood had soaked into the raw, uncovered wood of the floorboards, and the white sheets on the bed were stained a dull brownish red. On one of the walls they found a bloody palm print.

Maria Lucia stood in the doorway to the bedroom, and watched them.

ALEX **D**ELGADO, the one Puerto Rican detective on the squad, was home sick with the flu, so they called Patrolman Gomez upstairs from where he was watching television in the swing room on the ground floor, and asked him to interrogate the little girl. Gomez wanted to know what he should ask her. Just find out what happened, they told him. This is what happened:

GOMEZ: What were you doing alone in the house, querida-niña?
MARIA: I was waiting.
GOMEZ: For whom were you waiting?
MARIA: For Eduardo and Constantina. They went away.
GOMEZ: When did they go away?
MARIA: I don't know.
GOMEZ: Today?
MARIA: No.
GOMEZ: Then when? Last night? Yesterday?
MARIA: Many nights ago.
GOMEZ: How many nights ago?
MARIA: I don't know.
GOMEZ: She probably doesn't know how to count yet. Do you know how to count, Maria?
MARIA: Maria *Lucia*.
GOMEZ: Maria Lucia, sí, sí. Do you know how to count?

MARIA:	Yes. One, four, eight, two, seven.
GOMEZ:	She doesn't know how to count.
KLING:	Ask her was it Sunday night?
GOMEZ:	Was it Sunday night?
MARIA:	Yes, Sunday.
GOMEZ:	Very good, Maria.
MARIA:	Maria *Lucia*.
GOMEZ:	Maria Lucia, yes.
CARELLA:	Ask her if anybody else lives there.
GOMEZ:	Niña, who lives there in the house with you?
MARIA:	Eduardo and Constantina.
GOMEZ:	And who else?
MARIA:	No one.
GOMEZ:	Just those? Your mother and father?
MARIA:	My mother and father are with the angels.
GOMEZ:	Then who are Eduardo and Constantina? In what manner are you related?
MARIA:	Eduardo is my brother. And Constantina is my sister.
GOMEZ:	And they left on Sunday night?
MARIA:	Yes.
GOMEZ:	They left you all alone?
MARIA:	Yes.
GOMEZ:	Why did they do that, chiquilla?
MARIA:	The men.
GOMEZ:	What do you mean? What men?
MARIA:	The men who came.
GOMEZ:	There were men there Sunday night?
MARIA:	Yes.
GOMEZ:	What men?

MARIA:	I do not know.
GOMEZ:	How many in number?
MARIA:	I do not know.
GOMEZ:	Can you tell me their names? Did they call one to the other by name?
MARIA:	No.
GOMEZ:	What did they look like then?
MARIA:	I do not know.
GOMEZ:	You do not remember what they looked like?
MARIA:	I did not see them.
GOMEZ:	But they were there, is this not true?
MARIA:	Yes. They came to take Eduardo and Constantina.
GOMEZ:	But then, where were *you?* If you did not see them?
MARIA:	In the toilet.
GOMEZ:	They did not know you were in the toilet?
MARIA:	No. I was frightened. I kept very still.
GOMEZ:	Frightened of what, querida-niña?
MARIA:	The noise.
GOMEZ:	What noise did you hear?
MARIA:	Constantina was crying.
GOMEZ:	And what other noise?
MARIA:	Like in Loíza Aldea. The Fiesta de Santiago Apóstol.
CARELLA:	What's that? What'd she just say?
GOMEZ:	That's a festival they hold once a year, in July. They shoot off rockets to start the procession. Maria Lucia? Do you mean the rockets? Was the noise like that of

	the rockets?
MARIA:	Yes. Very like the rockets in Loíza Aldea.
KLING:	Christ! She heard those bastards gunning down her own brother and sister!
CARELLA:	Jesus!
KLING:	Ask her what Kingsley was doing there.
GOMEZ:	Kingsley?
CARELLA:	The man with the beard. Ask her what he was doing there.
GOMEZ:	Why was the bearded one in your house?
MARIA:	To talk. With Eduardo and Constantina.
GOMEZ:	Of what did they talk?
MARIA:	Of many things. I know not of what. I did not understand. They talked softly. There was no noise when the bearded one was there. The noise came later. I went into the toilet, and then came the noise.
KLING:	This is Thursday. Do you think she's been alone in that apartment since Sunday?
GOMEZ:	Have you left the house since that night?
MARIA:	No.
GOMEZ:	Did you call for help?
MARIA:	No.
GOMEZ:	Did you try to open the door?
MARIA:	No.
GOMEZ:	But why not, chiquilla?
MARIA:	I knew Eduardo and Constantina would come back.

THEY went back to the building that afternoon and questioned each of the tenants on each of the floors.

None of them had heard or seen a thing. The child Maria Lucia had described a noise "very like the rockets in Loíza Aldea," but no one in the building had heard anything. And this on a Sunday night, when it might have been expected that most people retired early after the weekend in preparation for Monday's work ahead.

The clubhouse of the Death's Heads was located in an abandoned building on the corner of Concord and 48th. Carella and Kling saw a runner entering the building minutes before they reached it. They knew their presence was being announced, but they weren't expecting trouble; the neighborhood street gangs, except for certain of them listed by Broughan as "sworn cop killers," rarely looked for hassles with the Law, and indeed made a great show of being honest, cooperative citizens. But Carella and Kling were stopped at the entrance to the building, anyway. The youth who stood in their path was wearing a Zapata mustache and a Swedish Army coat that had once been white but which was now so discolored by layers of dirt and grime that it looked as mottled as a poncho camouflaged for jungle warfare. He stood at the top of the stoop with his hands in his pockets, and looked down at the cops and said nothing, as though waiting for them to make the move that would declare them intruders on his turf. Carella lifted his foot onto the first step, and the boy at the top of the steps said, "That's it, man."

"Yeah? *What's* it, man?" Carella said.

"That's as far as you go."

"I'm a police officer," Carella said, and wearily flashed the tin.

"You got a warrant to enter these premises?" the boy asked.

"What's your name?" Kling said.

"My name is Pacho. You got a warrant to enter these premises?"

"We're looking for anyone who might have known Eduardo Portoles," Carella said. "Or his sister Constantina."

"You got a warrant to enter these premises?" Pacho said again.

"Looks like we got a broken record here, Steve," Kling said.

"You got a lease to *live* in these premises?" Carella said.

"What?" Pacho said.

"I said do you pay *rent* here?"

"No, we don't pay rent here. That still don't give you the right to . . ."

"Pacho, don't get me sore, okay?" Carella said. "It's a cold day, and I don't like being up here in Riverhead, and I don't need trouble from some punk who thinks he's Horatio at the bridge. Now just get the hell out of the way, and let us in there, before we start finding all kinds of things to charge you with. Okay, Pacho?"

"You understand, Pacho?" Kling said.

"*Who* at the bridge?" Pacho said.

The two detectives were already halfway up the steps. Both of them had opened the third buttons of their overcoats, providing easy access for right-handed draws just in case Pacho was carrying anything but his hands in the big pockets of that dirty Swedish Army coat, and just in case he was dumb enough to try pulling it. Pacho turned his back, his hands still in his pockets.

"I'll take you up," he said. "Otherwise you might get hurt."

He had rescued his pride, first by turning his back to show the huge gargoyle painted on the white coat in luminous black, red tongue lashing out like flame, the legend THE DEATH'S HEADS circling over it; had rescued it further by letting the detectives know that he was a powerful man without whose presence their safety could not be guaranteed. As far as Carella and Kling were concerned, it was all bullshit. Even the gargoyle on the back of the coat—and one of the garments found in Portoles' apartment had been an identical Swedish Army coat, with the identical gargoyle painted on its back—even that, though a pleasant departure from the expected skull-and-crossbones cliché, was total theatrical bullshit. With grimaces provoked partially by the paramilitary ritual Pacho was forcing them to observe (they themselves belonged to a paramilitary organization, but this fact did not occur to them at the moment), and partially by the stench of garbage and human excrement on the steps, they followed Pacho up to the second floor. Another young man in a Swedish Army coat stood at the top of the steps.

"Say it," he said to Pacho, asking for the password even though he undoubtedly recognized Pacho as one of the gang.

"The nutter is our dame," Pacho said, or at least something that sounded like that. It made no sense whatever to Carella.

"Who're these two?" the second Death's Head asked.

"Detectives Carella and Kling of the 87th Squad," Carella said. "Who are you?"

"True Blue."

"Nice to meet you," Carella said. "Where's True Green?"

"I didn't get the name from no damn cigarette," True Blue said.

"Where *did* you get it?" Kling asked, looking somewhat less than fascinated.

"Eduardo gave it to me. Because I was loyal."

"Eduardo in charge around here?" Kling asked.

"Yeah, but he ain't here right now," Pacho said.

"Are you expecting him back?"

The two boys exchanged a glance as transparent as a diamond. "Sure," Pacho said, "but we don't know when."

"We'll wait," Carella said.

"Anybody else we can talk to meanwhile?" Kling asked.

"Henry is here, he's the secretary."

"Well, let's talk to Henry then, okay?"

"Where *is* Henry?"

"In there," True Blue said, and gestured with his head toward a doorless jamb down the corridor.

"Would you like to announce us, or shall we go

right in?" Kling said.

"I better tell him you're here," Pacho said. "Otherwise you might get hurt."

Carella yawned. Pacho went up the corridor and disappeared into the room. True Blue kept looking at them.

"Any heat in this building?" Carella asked.

"No."

"Any water?"

"No. We don't need no heat or water. We're Death's Heads."

"Mmm," Carella said.

"We improvise."

"I'll bet you do," Carella said. "What's going on in there? Big conference about the fuzz from downtown?"

"I didn't *think* I recognized you from this precinct," True Blue said.

"You know all the detectives in this precinct?"

"Most of them. They know *me,* too."

"Mmm," Carella said, and Pacho came out into the hallway.

"Okay," Pacho said, "he'll see you."

"Nice of him," Kling said to Carella.

"Very nice," Carella answered.

The room they entered had been decorated with photographs of nude women clipped from various girlie magazines, and then varnished over to protect them. The walls were covered from floor to ceiling with these glossy cutouts, and various and several parts of the ladies' anatomies had been territorially claimed by different members of the gang, their names scrawled across breasts, buttocks, thighs, groins, and grinning mouths. In the midst of this pulchritudinous photographic display, sitting like a wizened priest on a fat red-velvet cushion, was a bespectacled young man wearing a Fu Manchu mustache and toying with a twelve-inch-long bread knife. Carella assumed the boy was Henry, and he further assumed that Henry was a fearless type; possession of such a utensil in circumstances such as these could presumably have led to a bust. Henry had known the cops were outside and coming in to pay a little visit; he could easily have tucked the blade under the fat pillow that cradled him.

"You're cops, huh?" he asked. He was delicately pressing one forefinger against the curved top of the knife's handle, the blade against the naked floorboards, trying to balance it on its tip. The knife refused to stay balanced. Each time it toppled over, he picked it up and tried again. He did not look up at the detectives as they came into the room.

"We're cops," Carella said.

"What do you want? We ain't done nothing."

"We want to know about Eduardo Portoles."

"He's the president."

"Where is he?"

"Out."

"Out where?"

"Big city, man," Henry said, and picked up the knife, and tried to balance it again, and again it fell over on its side. He had still not looked up at the detectives.

"How about Constantina Portoles?"

"Yeah, his sister."

"Know where she is?"

"Nope," Henry said, and the knife fell over again. He picked it up.

"She a member of the gang?"

"Yep."

"But you don't know where *she* is, either, right?"

"Right, man," Henry said, and tried his balancing act again. This time he came almost close. But the knife toppled over again. "Shit," he said, and still did not look up at the detectives.

"And the other sister?"

"What other one is that?" Henry asked.

"Maria Lucia. The *little* sister."

"What about her?"

"Got any idea where *she* is?"

"Nope," Henry said.

"*We* know where she is," Kling said.

"Yeah, where is she?"

"Right now she's at Washington Hospital, being treated for near-starvation."

"What?" Henry said, and looked up for the first time.

There was no disguising the genuine surprise in his eyes. If Carella was reading Henry's face correctly, then Henry did not know the little girl had escaped the Sunday-night massacre. That had to be it. No matter what Henry had read in the newspapers, he had automatically assumed that the killers had wiped out the entire Portoles family, including little Maria Lucia.

"That's right," Carella said, "she's in the hospital. And before that, she was up in the squadroom telling us all about what happened last Sunday night, when Eduardo and Constantina Portoles got killed."

"I don't know what you're talking about," Henry said. He was wearing thick glasses, and his eyes looked inordinately large behind them. Now that he was looking directly up at the detectives, he refused to take his eyes from them, as though this were as great a challenge as trying to balance the knife on its tip.

"What's the cover-up for?" Kling asked. "We're trying to find who killed them."

Henry did not answer.

"You *know* they're dead, for Christ's sake, you *had* to have seen those pictures in the paper."

"I didn't see nothing," Henry said.

"What're you going to do, Henry? Go after them yourself?"

"I ain't going to do nothing," Henry said.

"Are you the leader of this gang now?"

"I'm the secretary. I thought Pacho told you that."

"Pacho's full of shit, and so are you. You're the president now, or the acting president, or whatever the hell they choose to call you till they can elect a new one. Eduardo's dead, and if you don't know who did it, you've got some pretty strong suspicions. You're going to try to handle this yourself, aren't you?"

"I don't know anything," Henry said. "I got no suspicions about nothing."

"Murder's murder, Henry. Whether somebody *else* does it, or *you* do it, it's still murder."

"So?"

"He's saying keep your nose clean," Kling said. "Leave this to us. We're working on it, and we'll take care of it."

"Sure you will," Henry said.

"Be smart, Henry," Carella said. "Instead of causing a lot of trouble for yourself, why don't you help us?"

"I got no help to give you," Henry said.

"Okay, fine," Carella said. "We're heading over to Gateside Avenue, to talk to the Scarlet Avengers. Maybe they'll feel differently about it. Maybe they're not as dumb as you are." He turned his back on Henry and started for the door.

"They're even dumber," Henry said behind him.

WE got the bug from one of these mail-order catalogs. You can get all kinds of surveillance equipment just by sending away for it. We paid for the bug with funds from the clique's treasury. We put the bug in the Gateside clubhouse long before I ordered the double-hit, and we put it in because it was essential to know what the other side was doing. We tried to get a bug in the Heads' clubhouse, too, but their security was tighter. It was a good thing we had that bug on Gateside, though, because that was how we kept track of the Scarlets' movements. Also, we heard the whole conversation you guys had with their war counselor.

We sent three guys to put in the bug, all of them minors. The reason for that is we figured if they got caught, if the Scarlets decided to blow the whistle and bring charges or whatever, then you guys would be dealing with three little kids, you dig? Like the courts go easy on little kids. And we figured if just these little kids were involved, it would be considered nothing more than a caper, and also you wouldn't be able to hang nothing on the rest of us. Because we're of age, you see. We would have to pay if we got caught doing something like that. It's illegal, ain't it? Putting in a wire? Ain't that illegal? Anyway, that's what we figured, and that's why we sent Little Anthony and two other juniors. It wasn't easy, putting in that bug on Gateside, I can tell you. They took a tremendous risk. They did it because they knew our clique was trying to make peace, and that it was essential to get all the information we needed. Here's how we brought it off.

We stoned the building.

That was our diversion, to get the Scarlets out so we could get in. We already had the wire strung up over the roof. All we had to do was get in the clubhouse some way, and plant the bug. We done this just before Christmas. Man, we busted every window on the face of that building! Them Scarlets came running out of there, man, you'd think the place was on fire! They chased us up the block while meanwhile Little Anthony and the other two juniors rigged the wire. You know that big piece of cardboard they got nailed to the wall? With their club rules on it? They stuck the bug right behind their rules. I got such a laugh when they told me where they put it! That was adding insult to injury, am I right?

The bug was very valuable to us. It was through the bug that we found out the president of the Scarlets was staying home with his wife on the night we planned the hit. We didn't know they had a baby. Them Scarlets like to keep themselves secret and private, as if they got a lot to hide. The baby was just an accident. If we'd picked up anything about a baby on the bug, we probably would've tried to hit Atkins in the street. The hit wasn't designed to get no innocent bystanders. But you make a protective hit like that, you can't expect absolute accuracy all the time. Besides, like I told you, Chingo thinks maybe a wild shot from Atkins' own piece was what killed the kid. You should hear some of the stuff we picked up on that bug. I always knew those niggers were bums, but some of the things they done in their clubhouse were unbelievable. Dirty, you know what I mean? Just plain dirty.

The day you went to Gateside, I was listening personally. I heard the whole conversation you had with the Scarlets' war counselor, this guy who calls himself Mighty Man. He never wanted peace from the beginning. He kept *saying* he wanted peace, sure. But it was *his* kind of peace. And what kind of peace would that have been? Our clique wanted the kind of peace that would last forever. That's what we were trying to achieve. Right from the beginning. We didn't *create* what's in this neighborhood, you know. We inherited it. And it stunk, and we were trying to find a decent, honorable way out of it. If the Scarlets and the Heads had been trying to find the same kind of peace, we wouldn't be having all the trouble we've got now. I got nothing to be ashamed of. What I done was right. It was the *other* cliques who couldn't understand and who wouldn't cooperate. It's honor that was at stake. The clique's honor and my own honor as the president. But just try to explain that to some of these dopes.

Anyway, the day you went up there, I was listening. And it went just the way I figured it would. The Scarlets wouldn't have nothing to do with you, they wouldn't give you the right time of day. They knew who was responsible for what happened to their president, and they were going to take care of it by themselves, without no help from the fuzz. And I heard you when you told them you'd got the same reaction from this four-eyed kid Henry who's running the Heads, and I heard you when you said they were all being stupid and just asking for trouble. I don't like the Scarlets, and I don't trust none of them as far as I can throw them. But I got to admit they done the right thing that day when they told you to keep out of it, it was none of your business.

I didn't know at the time exactly *how* they planned to handle it, but I figured it would be some kind of retaliation strike. I wasn't worried. I knew we could take whatever the Scarlets and the Heads together had to dish out. We're a strong clique, man. We got the biggest arsenal in all Riverhead, second to none. There's a clique in Calm's Point just about as strong as us, but that's it in the whole city. We got the power, and we also got the restraint to know when to use it and when not. That's a big responsibility. When you left Gateside that day, I figured we wouldn't have no trouble from you, we wouldn't be linked in no way by anything either the Heads or the Scarlets had told you. We were clean and away, and we were capable of standing up to anything either of the two cliques could throw at us.

But that was before Midge made her second dumb move, and changed the picture entirely.

5

THE police in the bordering state found the body of the dead girl in a clump of woods outside the little town of Turman. Her throat had been slit from ear to ear, and her back was welted with what appeared to be marks left by a lash or a strap. An alert detective, recalling an all-points bulletin from across the river, noticed that the girl was wearing a wrist locket with the name MIDGE engraved on it. He checked his memory back at the office, and put in a call to the 87th Squad.

The River Harb was icebound almost shore-to-shore when Carella and Kling drove across the Hamilton Bridge early that Friday morning, January 11. Kling was driving. Carella was on the seat beside him, trying to adjust the heater in the ancient car. The automobile, one of the three assigned to the squad, had seen far better days. Either of the detectives would have preferred driving his own car, except that putting in chits for gasoline expenditures had become a big departmental hassle in recent weeks, and it was simpler to drive one of the assigned Police Department vehicles, which came equipped with a full tank of gas in the morning.

"I think I figured it out," Kling said.

"The whole case, or what?" Carella asked.

"What he meant."

"Who?"

"Pacho. When he took us up the stairs, and this other kid challenged him. Remember? True Blue, the other kid."

"Yes, I remember."

"He asked Pacho for the password, remember? And Pacho said, 'The nutter is our dame.' It's been bothering me, but I think I finally doped it out."

"Yeah?" Carella said.

"Yeah. They've got gargoyles painted on the backs of those white coats, am I right?"

"Uh-huh."

"Okay, so where do you find gargoyles?"

"On buildings."

"What kind of buildings?"

"*All* kinds of buildings."

"Steve, which building in the whole world is the most famous for its gargoyles?"

"I have no idea."

"Come on, you know the building."

"I do not know the building."

"Notre Dame," Kling said. Proud of his deductive feat, grinning, he turned his eyes momentarily to Carella. "You get it?" he said.

"No," Carella said.

"The nutter is our dame," Kling said, looking again at the road ahead. "The *notre* is our dame. You get it now?"

"That's ridiculous," Carella said.

"I'll bet it's what he meant."

"Okay, fine."

"Anyway, it was bothering me, and it's not any more."

"Good. What's wrong with this heater, would you happen to know that?"

"No. Something else has been bothering me, too, Steve."

"What? I know, don't tell me. You've been trying to learn how to balance a knife on the tip of its blade."

"No. It's Augusta. I'm thinking of asking her to marry me."

"Yeah?" Carella said, surprised.

"Yeah," Kling said, and nodded.

He was referring to Augusta Blair, a red-headed photographer's model he had met nine months ago while investigating a burglary. Carella knew better than to make some wise-ass remark when Kling was apparently so serious. The squadroom banter about the frequent calls from "Gussie" (as Kling's colleagues called her) had achieved almost monumental proportions in the past two months, but they hardly seemed appropriate in the one-to-one intimacy of an automobile whose windows, except for the windshield, were entirely covered with rime. Carella busied himself with the heater.

"What do you think?" Kling asked.

"Well, I don't know. Do you think she'll say yes?"

"Oh, yeah, I think she'll say yes."

"Well then, ask her."

"Well," Kling said, and fell silent.

They had come through the tollbooth. Behind them, Isola thrust its jagged peaks and minarets into a leaden sky. Ahead, the terrain consisted of rolling smoke-colored hills through which the road to Turman snaked its lazy way.

"The thing is," Kling said at last, "I'm a little scared."

"Of what?" Carella asked.

"Of getting married. I mean, it's . . . well . . . it's a very serious commitment, you know."

"Yes, I know," Carella said. He could not quite understand Kling's hesitancy. If he really wanted to marry Gussie, why the doubts? And if there were doubts, then did he really want to marry her?

"What's it like?" Kling asked.

"What's *what* like?"

"Being married."

"I can only tell you what it's like being married to Teddy," Carella said.

"Yeah, what's it like?"

"It's wonderful."

"Mmm," Kling said. "Because, suppose you get married and then you find out it isn't the same as when you weren't married?"

"*What* isn't the same?"

"Everything."

"Like what?"

"Like, well, for example, suppose, well, that, well, the sex isn't the same?"

"Why should it be any different?"

"I don't know," Kling said, and shrugged.

"What's the marriage certificate got to do with it?"

"I don't know," Kling said, and shrugged again. "*Is* it the same? The sex?"

"Sure," Carella said.

"I don't mean to get personal . . ."

"No, no."

"But it's the same, huh?"

"Sure, it's the same."

"And the rest? I mean, you know, do you still have fun?"

"Fun?"

"Yeah."

"Sure, we have fun."

"Like before?"

"Better than before."

"Because we have a lot of fun together," Kling said. "Augusta and I. A lot of fun."

"That's good," Carella said.

"Yes, it's very good. That two people can enjoy things together. I think that's very good, Steve, don't you?"

"Yes, I think it's very good when that happens between two people."

"Not that we don't have fights," Kling said.

"Well, everybody has fights. Any two people . . ."

"Yes, but not too many."

"No, no."

"And our . . . our personal relationship is very good. We're very good together."

"Mmm."

"The sex, I mean," Kling said quickly, and suddenly seemed very intent on the road ahead. "That's very good between us."

"Mmm, well, good. That's good."

"Though not always. I mean, sometimes it's not as good as other times."

"Yes, well, that's natural," Carella said.

"But *most* of the time . . ."

"Yes, sure."

"Most of the time, we really do enjoy it."

"Sure," Carella said.

"And we love each other. That's important."

"That's the single most important thing," Carella said.

"Yes, I think so."

"No question."

"It *is* the single most important thing," Kling said. "It's what makes everything else seem right. The decisions we make together, the things we do together, even the fights we have together. It's the fact that we love each other . . . well . . . that's what makes it *work,* you see."

"Yes," Carella said.

"So you think I should marry her?"

"It sounds like you're married already," Carella said.

Kling turned abruptly from the wheel to see whether or not Carella was smiling. Carella was not. He was hunched on the seat with his feet propped up against the clattering heater, and his hands tucked under his arms, and his chin ducked into the upturned collar of his coat.

"I suppose it *is* sort of like being married," Kling said, turning his attention to the road again. "But not exactly."

"Well, how's it any different?" Carella said.

"Well, I don't know. That's what I'm asking you."

"Well, I don't see any difference."

"Then why should we get married?" Kling asked.

"Jesus, Bert, *I* don't know," Carella said. "If you want to get married, get married. If you don't, then stay the way you are."

"Why'd *you* get married?"

Carella thought for a long time. Then he said, "Because I couldn't bear the thought of any other man ever touching Teddy."

Kling nodded.

He said nothing more all the way to Turman.

THE detective's name was Al Grundy. He first took them to the hospital mortuary to show them the girl's body, and then he drove them out to where the corpse had been found. The initial discovery had been made by two teen-age boys cutting through the woods on their way to school. One of them had stayed with the dead girl, nervously waiting some ten feet from where the body lay partially covered with leaves that had fallen in October and were now moldering and wet. The other had raced to the nearest pay telephone and called the police, who responded within four minutes. There were tire tracks in the wet leaves, and it was assumed that the body had been transported to this isolated glade from someplace else.

"Think it's the girl you're looking for?" Grundy asked.

He was a huge black-haired man with light-blue eyes, freckles spattered across the bridge of his nose. He could not have been older than twenty-five or -six. Standing beside him, Kling suddenly felt ancient, suddenly felt it was time he *did* get married, and had kids, and became a grandfather.

"Maybe," Carella said. "Have you got a last name for her? Was she carrying any identification?"

"Nothing but the locket on her wrist."

"No handbag?"

"Nothing."

"Any houses nearby?"

"Just the one over the knoll there. Doubt if anyone could've seen anything from there. Because of the way the ground slopes."

"The road we came in on, is that the only access road?"

"Yeah. Route 14. We traced the tire tracks back to where they must've drove in," Grundy said. "The mud and the leaves made that easy. But there's nothing on the road itself that would indicate which direction they came from."

"What about the kids who found her? Have you talked to them?"

"Oh, yeah. They're clean, I think. You never can tell, but these kids had two things going for them: one, they called the cops, and two, they both looked scared shitless."

"What'd the coroner have to say about the time of death?"

"Set it at sometime between ten and twelve P.M. last night. She'd been beaten badly, bleeding welts across her back, looked like somebody whipped her before cutting her throat. No sexual assault. Vaginal vault is clean of semen."

"Mind if we talk to the people in the house up there?"

"Be my guest," Grundy said.

The "people" in the house up there turned out to be only one person. His name was Rodney Sack, and he was seventy-six years old, and he appeared very frightened by the appearance of detectives in his kitchen. He was just sitting down to breakfast, and was wearing blue denim coveralls, a wool plaid sports shirt, a blue cardigan sweater threadbare at the elbows, and a hearing aid. The hearing aid did not help matters much. His obvious fear made matters even worse.

The detectives were trying to find out exactly who "Midge" was. They had gone through Broughan's gang files quite thoroughly, and had found no such nickname for any girl-auxiliary member. The scrutiny had not been a simple one; there were records on 153 gangs in West Riverhead alone. The Scarlet Avengers and the Death's Heads had been involved in hostile combat with many of those gangs since their respective formations three and four years back. Picking out the gang that had decided to do in the leaders of the

Avengers and the Heads was rather like picking a dish at a Chinese banquet: everything looked good. So far, the detectives had only two leads. They knew that Andrew Kingsley had been with Eduardo and Constantina Portoles for some time before a person or persons unknown had entered the apartment and killed all three of them. They did not know why Kingsley had been there, or what his relationship with Portoles and his sister had been. They also knew that a girl named Midge, presumably an auxiliary member of the rampaging gang, had supplied them with information, and then had turned up in the next state, two days later, with her throat slit. But who the hell was Midge?

"Notice any unusual traffic in the woods down there last night?" Carella asked Sack.

"No, sir," Sack said, visibly trembling.

"Any headlights or anything?"

"What would red lights be doing down there in—"

"Headlights. *Head*lights. Automobile headlights."

"Oh, headlights," Sack said. "No, didn't see no headlights down there." He tried to light his pipe, and the match fell from his shaking hand. He took another wooden match from the box of kitchen matches, and broke the match striking it. He looked up at the detectives, smiled weakly, and put the pipe aside.

"What are you scared of, Mr. Sack?" Kling asked.

"Me? Nothing. What've I got to be scared of?"

"Did you see something down in those woods last night?"

"No, sir, I did not."

"Where *were* you last night, Mr. Sack?" Carella

said, and realized that both he and Kling were shouting at the old man. Carella's wife was a deaf-mute, and he never thought of her inability to hear or speak as an affliction. But Sack's partial deafness was inordinately irritating. Carella suddenly realized that *most* people were annoyed by the partially deaf, whereas their patience was normally quite generous toward the partially blind, or the crippled. He put the thought aside, certain he would discuss it later with Teddy, her eyes watching his lips intently, her fingers answering in the deaf-mute language they shared, and which he "spoke" fluently and with a distinctive accent all his own. Sack was staring up at him. He was not sure the old man had heard him. "Mr. Sack, where were you . . . ?"

"I heard you, I heard you," Sack said impatiently, and Carella now saw the other side of the coin, the annoyance of the hard-of-hearing at being subjected to shouting and repetition and constant doubt as to whether they heard what was being said to them.

"Well, where were you?"

"Here."

"All night?"

"All night, yes."

"What were you doing between ten o'clock and midnight?"

"Sleeping."

"What time did you go to bed?"

"Nine o'clock. I go to bed nine o'clock every night."

"Hear anything unusual down there in the woods?" Kling asked.

"I'm hard of hearing," Sack said with great dignity. "I wouldn't have heard a cannon if it went off on the porch."

"Did you get out of bed any time during the night?"

"Well, yes, I suppose so."

"When?"

"Don't remember exactly when. Had to go to the toilet, so I got out of bed."

"Where's the toilet?" Carella asked.

"Back of the house."

"Overlooking the woods?"

"Yes."

"Is there a window in the toilet?"

"Yes."

"Did you look out that window while you were in there?"

"Don't recall as I did."

"*Try* to recall," Kling said.

"I suppose I might've glanced out there."

"What'd you see?"

"The woods."

"Anything in the woods?"

"Trees, bushes." Sack shrugged.

"Anything else?"

"Animals maybe. Lots of deer come close to the house, foraging."

"*Did* you see any animals last night?"

"Well, yes, I suppose so."

"What *kind* of animals?"

"Well, hard to say. Pretty dark out there except for the . . ." Sack stopped in midsentence.

"Except for the *what?*" Carella said.

"Porch light," Sack said. "Always keep the porch light on."

"By the porch, do you mean that porch on the front of the house?"

"Yes, that's the porch."

"Is there a back porch, Mr. Sack?"

"No, just that front porch there."

"But you said the toilet is at the *back* of the house."

"Well, yes. Yes, that's where it is."

"Then what's the light on the *front* porch got to do with what you saw or didn't see from the *back?*"

Sack blinked, and then suddenly began crying. "I'm an old man," he said, and fumbled for a handkerchief in the pocket of his coveralls. "I can't hear worth a shit, and I'm living on my disability pension and what I get from the welfare. I got maybe five, six years left of living, if that much. I don't want trouble. Please leave me alone. Please." He blew his nose and dabbed at his eyes, and then put the handkerchief away, even though tears were still running down his cheeks. "Please," he said.

"Want to tell us what happened last night, Mr. Sack?" Carella said gently.

"Nothing," Sack said. "I already told you . . ." He could not go on. A sob strangled the sentence, and he began coughing, and again reached for his handkerchief.

"*Did* you see headlights down there in the woods, Mr. Sack?"

Sack did not answer.

"Yes or no?"

"I saw headlights," he said, and sighed heavily. "I'm an old man. Please, I don't want trouble."

"What time was this, Mr. Sack? The headlights."

"Must've been about two in the morning."

"You saw them from the bathroom window?"

"Yes."

"What'd you do?"

"I should've gone back to bed, but I thought . . . I thought somebody maybe got off the road by accident . . . and was stuck in the mud down there by the bottom, so I . . . I put on a pair of pants and a shirt, and my sweater and my lumberjack, and I went down there to see if . . . if I could offer some assistance. Phone a garage or . . . I'm an old man, and I'm deaf, but I ain't worthless. I have some value, you see. I thought I could phone, if the people down there needed help."

"Go on," Kling said. He said the two words quite softly, and was not at all sure that Sack heard them.

"I wasn't carrying no light, I looked for the damn flashlight, but I couldn't find it. I keep losing things around here, I don't know what it is. But there was a pretty good moon, and I know those woods like the back of my hand, I was born and raised in this house, I know every inch of them woods. And I made my way down to where the lights were, and . . . and then I saw what was going on."

"What was that, Mr. Sack?"

"I said I saw what was going on."

"Yes, and what did you see?"

"There was a girl laying on the ground in front of the truck. There was blood all over her dress. There was two young boys standing in the headlights near her. They were having an argument."

"What about?"

"One of them wanted to bury her. He said they'd brought along the shovels so they could bury her. The other one said he wanted to get out of there fast, it was good enough what they'd already done, covered her with leaves."

"What'd they look like?"

"They were just kids, couldn't've been older than sixteen or seventeen."

"White or black?"

"White."

"Did they use names in addressing each other? Did you hear any names?"

"I'm hard of hearing," Sack said again, "but I think I heard one of them calling the other one 'Pig.'"

"Pig? P-I-G?"

"That's right. Pig."

"Are you *sure* that's what he said?"

"I'm not sure, no. But that's what it sounded like to me."

"All right, what happened?"

"The one named Pig said he was in charge, and he didn't want to spend no more time there in the woods. So they got in the truck and drove off."

"What kind of truck?"

"Old Chevy pickup."

"Notice the license plate?"

"It was an Isola plate, but I couldn't make out the numbers on it."

"When you say old . . . what year do you mean?"

"Sixty-four, sixty-five, something like that."

"What color?"

"Green, it looked like. Or blue. A bluish-green."

"An open pickup?"

"Yes."

"Anything in the back of the truck?"

"Nothing I could see. I guess there were shovels in it, because that's what they were talking about. But I couldn't see them from where I was."

"Anything else you remember about the truck? Any dents, any peculiar markings, anything painted on its sides?"

"There was a funny flag painted on the door closest to me."

"Which door was that?"

"The door on the driver's side."

"What kind of flag?"

"I couldn't make it out. I *think* it was a flag, it looked like a flag, anyway."

"What color was it?"

"Red, white, and blue."

"But it wasn't an American flag?"

"No, no, I *know* what the American flag looks like, don't I? This had a big blue cross on it. Stars, too, now that you mention it. But it wasn't the Stars and Stripes, that's for sure. I fought for that flag, I sure as hell ought to know what it looks like. World War I. That's how come I'm deaf."

"What'd these boys look like, can you tell us that?"

"Both had dark hair, and both were wearing blue jackets with . . . Hey, that's right. That's *right,* come to think of it."

"*What's* right, Mr. Sack?"

"That same flag was on the back of their jackets. That's right. Same damn flag."

"Uh-huh. How tall were they?"

"Average height."

"Notice anything else about them? Scars or . . . ?"

"Yeah, one of them *was* wearing a scarf."

Carella did not mention that he had said "Scars."

Instead, he picked up on the old man's recollection, and said, "What color was the scarf?"

"Red."

"Which one was wearing it? Pig or the other one?"

"I don't recall."

"Any other identifying marks?" Carella said, and then amended his earlier question so that Sack wouldn't realize he had misheard it. "Any disfigurations? Old healed wounds? Anything like that?"

"Scars, do you mean?" Sack said.

Carella smiled. "Yes, Mr. Sack," he said. "Scars."

"No. No scars. Oh, is *that* what you meant before? Oh, I see. No. No scars." Sack, for some strange reason, was smiling too.

"Thank you, Mr. Sack," Carella said. "I wouldn't worry about those two coming back here. They've no reason to believe they were seen by anyone. They didn't see *you,* did they?"

"No, but . . . I figured if I told you about it, they might

guess where the information came from and . . . that girl's *dead,* you know. It don't take a mastermind to dope out it was them two who did it."

"If it'll make you feel more secure, I'm sure Detective Grundy can arrange to have his men tighten the patrol around your place. Mr. Grundy?"

"Oh, sure," Grundy said, taken by surprise and not at all sure he *could* ask his men to provide such a service.

"You've been very helpful, Mr. Sack," Carella said. "We're sorry to have interrupted your breakfast."

"We're grateful," Kling said.

"Don't care for it," Sack said. "Too bitter."

IN the squadroom of the One-Oh-One, they went through Broughan's file again. They learned that there was a gang called, in seeming contradiction, the Yankee Rebels. Their colors were red, white, and blue, and their identifying insignia was the same one the Confederacy had used during the War Between the States—the distinctive blue cross with its thirteen white stars and white edges against a field of red. The names and nicknames (called "aliases" in Broughan's file) of the gang members were included in the dossier, together with pertinent facts about them—family make-up, school and/or employment histories, records of arrests and convictions, probation and/or parole dispositions, and the like. One of the members of the Yankee Rebels was called Little Anthony, apparently in an attempt to distinguish him from Big Anthony, who was listed as the gang's treasurer. The detectives assumed that what Rodney Sack had heard on the night of Midge's murder was not the name "Pig," but rather the name "Big," short for Big Anthony Sutherland. The legal name of the gang's "enforcement officer" was Charles Ingersol; his nickname was Chingo. The gang's negotiator was a boy named Edward Marshall, but he was called Doc because he had once dug a bullet (with apparent success) from the shoulder of a fellow member who'd been wounded in a street fight. The gang's war counselor was named Edward Mason, and *his* nickname was Mace.

The president's name was Randall M. Nesbitt.

He was known to his followers as Randy.

6

WHAT happened was she tried to get away.

They had her word of honor that she wouldn't try to pull anything like that, but if you can't trust somebody once, then you certainly can't trust them twice. I always believed, by the way (and I *still* believe), that there's no such thing as trusting somebody only halfway, or three-quarters of the way, or even ninety-nine and one-hundredths percent of the way. You either trust them completely, or you're not trusting them at all. Which is why in all these peace negotiations, I was the one who insisted that everything be spelled out to the letter. Otherwise, we'd have had to depend on trust, you see, and I don't trust neither the Heads nor the Scarlets as far as I can throw them.

The house Big Anthony's aunt has is really more like a cottage. There's only one bedroom, so Big Anthony and Jo-Jo, who's the guy he picked to go with him, gave the bedroom to Midge, and they slept in the living room, Big Anthony on the couch and Jo-Jo on the floor in a sleeping bag. They never made no sexual advances to Midge because they knew she was Johnny's girl, and they know this clique prides itself on its honor. They stripped her to the waist every morning and every night to give her the prescribed twenty lashes, but that had nothing to do with sex. That was only a sentence being carried out. It really must have bothered Big Anthony to carry out such a sentence against a girl, because this clique truly honors the women who belong to it. In our eyes, they are equal members and they are entitled to equal rights. Just because I didn't appoint any of them as my advisers don't mean nothing. Before this thing with Midge happened, I was *planning* to appoint one of the girls as secretary. I was ready to bring it before the council, in fact. Then Midge had to get smart. Or *stupid,* if you want to be exact about it.

It was right after they gave her that night's twenty. She was bleeding a little, but not much. She put on her blouse and went in the bedroom. Big Anthony told me she never made a peep while they were administering justice. He thought she'd learned her lesson. He thought she'd got the message, just the way *I* thought she had. Neither of us had made a mistake; it was just that Midge was a very devious person. Along about nine-thirty Big and Jo-Jo were watching television in the living room, and they had the sound very low so as not to disturb Midge if she was trying to sleep, when they heard something outside that sounded like somebody trying to get in the house. Jo-Jo ran around one side, and Big ran around the other, and it wasn't nobody trying to get *in* the house, it was somebody trying to get *out* of the house. It was Midge, in fact, and not only was she *trying* to get out, she was *already* out by the time they ran around back and caught her. She had jumped out the window (which was the noise they heard) and had started for the woods by the time they got to her, and she was carrying a knife she had managed to steal from the kitchen earlier in the day.

Neither Jo-Jo nor Big had any intention of hurting her. All they wanted to do was get her back in the house. But she came at them with the knife in her hand, and she stabbed Jo-Jo in the arm (he's *still* got a bandage where she cut him) and then she went after Big, who ain't called Big for nothing, and who's been in enough fights to know how to take a weapon away from somebody. But she kept slashing at *him,* too, and by the time he got the knife away, he was beginning to lose his temper. He grabbed her from behind, with one arm holding her, you know, and he put the blade against her throat, and he told her one more move and he'd kill her. She turned halfway around, and she kicked him in the balls, and that was what did it. Big killed her on the spot. He had good reason.

I told him he done the right thing.

THEY did not find Randall Nesbitt until Saturday morning, January 12, in an ice cream parlor on the corner of Hitchcock and Dooley in Riverhead. He was eating a banana split. A skinny, light-eyed blond girl was sitting in the booth opposite him, drinking a chocolate ice cream soda. She looked shy, somewhat anemic, and somewhat anachronistic, as though she had stepped out of a Betty Co-ed movie of the forties. Nesbitt himself had dark hair and dark brooding eyes and a sloping, bulbous nose, and heavy jowls, and apparently a heavy beard as well; he looked as though he had recently shaved, but a bluish cast tinted his jaw and both sides of his face below the cheeks. He did not look up when the detectives approached the booth. He had undoubtedly known they were coming because they had seen a runner, wearing a blue denim jacket with the Confederate insignia on its back, entering the ice cream parlor as they came up the street. The runner was now sitting at the counter. He watched the detectives as they stopped before the booth.

"Randall Nesbitt?" Carella asked.

"Um?" Nesbitt said, and looked up. There was a smile on his face—the expansive, calculated smile of a television celebrity on a late-night show.

Carella distrusted the smile at once. "Police officers," he said, and flashed the tin.

Nesbitt studied the gold-and-blue shield with great interest, and then looked up and smiled again. "Yes, Officer," he said, "how can I help you?"

"What's *your* name, young lady?" Kling asked.

"Toy," the girl said.

"Toy?"

"Toy Wilke."

"We'd like to ask you a few questions," Carella said to Nesbitt. "Mind if we sit down?"

"Please join us," Nesbitt said. "Would you like some ice cream? Or a cup of coffee or something?"

"Thank you, no," Carella said, and sat in the booth alongside Toy. Kling sat next to Nesbitt. "Are you the president of a gang called the Yankee Rebels?" Carella asked across the table.

"That's the name of our clique, that's correct," Nesbitt said.

"We're trying to locate somebody named Midge," Carella said. "Would the name happen to register?"

Toy seemed about to say something, but a sidelong glance from Nesbitt silenced her.

"Midge," Nesbitt said thoughtfully, and tented his hands, and considered the name as though he'd just been invited to christen a battleship. "Midge, Midge," he said. "No, can't say that it rings a bell, Officer."

"We have information that leads us to believe Midge belongs to your gang."

"Really?" Nesbitt said. "Toy, you know any member named Midge?"

"No," Toy said, and bent over her glass, and put the straws between her lips, and busied herself with the soda.

"Sorry we can't help you," Nesbitt said. Then, as though to emphasize his dismissal of the two men, he picked up his spoon, cut into the banana with it, scooped a combination of chocolate sauce and cherry syrup into the bowl of the spoon, and shoveled the entire dripping mixture into his mouth.

"We're not quite finished yet," Carella said.

"Oh, sorry," Nesbitt said, swallowing. He put the spoon down again, smiled his eager, pleasant, cooperative smile, and said, "Yes?"

"Anyone in your gang named Big Anthony?"

"Why, yes," Nesbitt said.

"Know where we can find him?"

"Have you tried his house?"

"If you're referring to the apartment he shares with his mother, at 334 North 38th, yes, we've tried his house."

"I guess he wasn't there."

"That's right."

"I don't know where he is," Nesbitt said, and picked up the spoon again. He was dipping it into a melting scoop of strawberry ice cream when Carella said, "Does he have a driver's license?"

"Who? Big? Sure, he does."

"What kind of car does he drive?"

"He doesn't have a car."

"But the gang has a car."

"No, we don't have a car."

"Do you have a pickup truck?"

"Yes, we have a pickup truck," Nesbitt said. "You'll excuse me, Officer, but I'm not sure I understand where this line of questioning is going to."

"Stick around," Kling said.

Nesbitt smiled. "I wasn't going no place, Officer."

"That's right, you weren't," Kling said. "Not till we're through with you."

"Of course," Nesbitt said, "I know my rights, and—"

"Save it," Kling said curtly.

"I was going to say that maybe you ought to start advising me of them. I mean, if this is going to be a big interrogation scene here, then how about—?"

"This is a field interrogation, and your rights aren't in jeopardy," Kling said. "What kind of pickup truck do you own?"

"A Chevy."

"What year?"

"Sixty-four."

"Where is it now?"

"I don't know which one of the members has it right this minute," Nesbitt said, and smiled. "We're all allowed to drive it when we need it. All of us who've got licenses, of course. We're a law-abiding club."

"Who was driving it last time you saw it?" Carella asked.

"I forget."

"Try to remember."

"Why is it important?"

"It may have figured in an armed robbery," Kling lied.

"Really?" Nesbitt said. He shook his head. "I think you've got the wrong truck in mind."

"Greenish-blue, sixty-four Chevy with a Confederate flag painted on the driver's side."

"*Both* sides," Nesbitt said.

"The garage attendant only saw the driver's side," Carella said, picking up and amplifying Kling's lie.

"Gee," Nesbitt said, "maybe somebody stole our truck, eh, Toy?"

"Maybe," Toy said, and slurped up chocolate soda from the bottom of the glass.

"Because none of our guys, you see, would go holding up no gas station."

"But it does sound like your truck, doesn't it?"

"Oh, yeah, it *sounds* like it, all right. But it can't be, you see. Unless, like I said, the truck was stolen. We usually park it in the empty lot on Dill, near the clubhouse. Maybe somebody stole it, and then later went and stuck up a gas station."

"That's possible, Steve," Kling said.

"Yes, it's possible," Carella said.

"Sure, that's what must've happened," Nesbitt said. "I'd better get back to the clubhouse and check on it. There's supposed to be a man watching that truck at all times."

"Big Anthony's mother said he was out of town," Carella said abruptly.

"Yeah, well, she hardly ever knows *where* he is," Nesbitt said, and smiled.

"She seemed pretty certain about it."

"Well," Nesbitt said, and spread his hands in a gesture indicating Big Anthony's mother was not a competent or reliable witness.

"Said he left the apartment Wednesday night. Told her he might be gone a week or so."

"That's news to me, all right," Nesbitt said. "Officers, I have to tell you that's news to me. I'm president of this clique, and most of the members keep in touch with me concerning where they're going or not going. That's not a rule, you understand, they ain't *required* to keep me informed. But they do, and I usually know where they are. And Big never said a word to me about going out of town."

"His mother said he was going to Turman."

"Yeah? Across the river? Well, that's news to me."

"The reason we're so curious about Big Anthony is that the gas station that was held up happens to be in Turman."

"Officers," Nesbitt said, "I think you're lying to me. I don't know *why* you're lying, but I think you are."

"That makes us even," Kling said.

"Me? Are you talking about *me?*" Nesbitt said. "I never lie. I make a practice of always telling the truth."

"Good, so start telling it now," Carella said.

"I've been telling it all along."

"Where's Midge?"

"I don't know anybody named Midge."

"Where's Big Anthony?"

"I don't know. If his mother says he went to Turman, then maybe that's where he is, though his mother is a little nuts, and I frankly wouldn't trust her as far as I can throw her. But if she says he went to Turman, then who knows? Maybe for once in her lifetime she got something right, who knows?"

"*Where* in Turman?"

"He didn't even tell me he was going to Turman, so how would I know *where* he was going in Turman?"

"Have you heard from him since Wednesday?"

"Nope."

"Isn't that a little odd?"

"It's not a requirement that everybody has to tell me every time he's going to the bathroom," Nesbitt said. "I got good people, and they're free agents. They know I'm the president, and what I say goes, but they don't have to report to me every ten minutes."

"We're not talking about ten minutes. We're talking about three days. Are you trying to tell us that one of your members has been gone for three days, and you don't know anything about it?"

"That's not only what I'm *trying* to tell you, it's what I *am* telling you."

"We think Big Anthony and Midge are together."

"Impossible."

"Why?"

"First of all, who's Midge? If *I* don't know her, how would Big know her? And second of all, Big has a girl friend, and she would get very irritated if he was fooling around with some other chick. Isn't that right, Toy? Wouldn't she get very irritated?"

"Yeah," Toy said, "she would get very irritated."

The two detectives were watching Nesbitt intently. They had given him enough rope and he had hanged himself, and now they simply watched him silently, waiting for him to realize that the trap had sprung, and the noose had tightened around his neck, and his feet were dangling in the air over the scaffold.

"What's the matter?" Nesbitt said. "What are you looking at?"

Neither of the detectives answered.

"Must be a staring contest," Nesbitt said, and picked up his spoon. "This is all melting," he said to Toy, ignoring the detectives.

"How do you know she's a girl?" Carella said.

"Who? Who're you talking about now?" Nesbitt said.

"Same person. Midge. How do you know she's a girl?"

"You *said* she was a girl. You said you were looking for a girl named Midge."

"We said we were trying to locate *somebody* named Midge. We didn't say she was a girl."

"I figured she was a girl," Nesbitt said, and shrugged.

"What do you figure Chingo is?"

"A boy."

"But you figured Midge was a girl."

"That's right."

"Just like that, huh? Midge is automatically a girl."

"Automatically."

"Okay," Carella said, "we're going to level with you, Randy," and then immediately told another lie. "We're looking for Midge because we think she was an accomplice in a crime we're investigating."

"What crime is that?" Nesbitt said.

"A routine mugging. We think Midge and two boys hit an old lady on Peterson Drive."

"I wish I could help you," Nesbitt said, "but I don't

know her." They watched his face. Not a flicker of emotion flashed on it. If he already knew the girl was dead, if he'd received a call from Big Anthony in Turman, nothing in his dark brooding eyes revealed it.

"We don't think Big Anthony's involved," Kling said, embroidering the lie. "But somebody told us Midge was his girl. I guess our information was wrong there, Steve," he said, turning to Carella.

"I guess so. Randy says Big Anthony already *has* a girl. Isn't that right, Randy?"

"That's right."

"What's her name?"

"Ellie Nelson."

"Know where she lives?"

"Sure. On Dooley, two blocks from the clubhouse."

"What's the address?"

"1894 Dooley."

"And the apartment number?"

"5A. She won't know where Big Anthony is, either."

"How can you be sure?"

Nesbitt smiled his late-night, television-personality smile again. "I can be sure," he said.

O N the way up to the fifth floor of 1894 Dooley, Kling suddenly said, "I think I figured it out."

"What'd you figure out this time?"

"What he meant."

"Who? Nesbitt?"

"No, Sack. The old man in Turman."

"Sack?" Carella said. "That was *yesterday,* for God's sake."

"That's right, it's been bothering me. You remember when we were saying goodbye to him?"

"Yes?"

"And you thanked him and then apologized for having interrupted his breakfast?"

"Uh-huh."

"And I said 'We're grateful.' Do you remember that? And he answered 'Don't care for it. Too bitter.' I finally figured out what he meant."

"What did he mean?"

"Well, what was he doing when we went in there, Steve?"

"He was eating his breakfast."

"Right. And what do people have for breakfast?"

"All *kinds* of things, Bert."

"Yes, but what do they *start* with? What do *you* start with?"

"Juice."

"Yes, but not everybody starts with juice. Some people start with grapefruit."

"So?"

"So Sack thought I was talking about grapefruit. He misheard me. He thought 'grateful' was 'grapefruit.' That's why he answered 'Don't care for it. Too bitter.'" Kling smiled. "You get it, Steve?"

"That's ridiculous," Carella said.

"I'll bet it's what he meant."

"Okay, fine."

"Anyway, it was bothering me, and it's not any more."

"Good, here we are," Carella said, and stopped

before the door to 5A, and knocked on it.

Ellie Nelson was wearing a navy-blue T-shirt and dungaree pants when she opened the door. She was perhaps seventeen years old, quite pretty, with a pert nose and vibrant blue eyes. Her figure was good, and she knew it. She smiled up at the policemen as though she'd been expecting them. Carella and Kling assumed Nesbitt had telephoned her from the phone booth in the ice cream parlor.

"Hi," she said.

"Police officers," Carella said, and showed his shield. The girl barely glanced at it. "All right if we come in?"

"Sure, why not?" she said, and stepped away from the door, allowing them to enter the apartment. A gray-haired woman with a lace shawl over her shoulders was sitting by the kitchen window, rocking in a green rocking chair and knitting in a shaft of sunlight. Ellie caught the brief shifting of Kling's eyes, and said, "My grandmother. She won't bother us. Come in, come in."

"Anybody else live here in this apartment?" Kling asked.

"My mother, my grandmother, and me," Ellie said, and closed the door behind them. "Come on in the parlor. What'd you want?"

The living room was furnished in a three-piece suite done in red velveteen. A television set rested on a wheeled cart. There were no pictures or photographs on the walls. There was a curtain only on the window facing the street. The airshaft window had been left uncovered, and faced a grimy brick wall. Ellie sat in one of the easy chairs and gestured to the sofa. The detectives sat opposite her. "So, what'd you want?" she asked again.

"We understand you're Big Anthony's girl friend," Carella said.

"That's right," Ellie said, and smiled.

"That would be Anthony Sutherland, is that right?"

"That's right, Big Anthony. We call him that 'cause he's six feet four inches tall, and he's got shoulders this wide," Ellie said.

"And he's a member of the Yankee Rebels, is that also right?"

"That's right. Me, too. The women's auxiliary. It's a great clique. I only joined it 'cause I was going with Big Anthony, you know, and he's the treasurer. But, man, am I glad I did! It was really boring before I got involved with the Rebs. Life, I mean. You could go out of your mind with school around here, and nothing to do nights but sit and watch television. The Rebs changed all that. Well, Big Anthony, of course. But the Rebs, too. They're a real decent bunch of guys and girls, I mean it. They're the closest friends I've got in the world."

"Midge, too?" Carella asked abruptly.

Ellie's face went blank. "Midge?" she said.

"Midge. Red-headed girl, about five feet two inches tall, weight about ninety-seven, freckles across the bridge of her nose, wears a little gold locket on her wrist, heart-shaped, with the name Midge on it."

"Don't know her," Ellie said, and shrugged.

"We thought she was a member of the Yankee Rebels," Carella said.

"Never heard of her," Ellie said.

"Okay, when's the last time you saw your boy friend?"

"Wednesday afternoon," Ellie said.

"Where?"

"He came up here."

"And you haven't seen him since?"

"No."

"Do you know where he is?"

"No."

"When he was up here, did he mention that he might be leaving the city?"

"No."

"How long have you been going with him?"

"Close to a year."

"Has he called you since Wednesday?"

"No."

"Been going with him for a year, and he didn't mention he was leaving the city, and he hasn't called you since he left? Is that what you're asking us to believe, Ellie?"

"It's the truth," Ellie said, and shrugged again. "Why do you want him?"

"We think he's with this girl Midge," Kling said, and watched her carefully.

"Big?" she said. "Is with . . . this girl, whoever she is?"

"That's what we think."

"No," Ellie said, and shook her head. "You're mistaken. Big and I are going together, you see. We're almost like engaged. I mean, we plan to get married, you see. What would he be doing with . . . her?"

"With Midge."

"Yeah. Whatever her name is."

"Midge. That's her name. Very pretty little girl, from what we understand."

"Well, Big Anthony wouldn't . . . I mean, he just wouldn't go off with another girl. I mean, where would he go? And anyway, he wouldn't."

"To Turman, that's where he'd go."

"Turman?"

"Yes. Across the river."

"Well . . . what makes you think he went to Turman?"

"His mother said so. He left Wednesday night."

"Mrs. Sutherland said that?"

"That's what she said."

"That Big Anthony went to Turman?"

"Yes."

The girl fell silent. It was apparent (assuming Randy had indeed phoned to alert her) that he had not mentioned the possibility of the detectives' lying to her as they had lied to him. Ellie was biting her lower lip now, and thinking very hard about what they had just suggested—the possibility that *her* boy friend had left on Wednesday night for someplace across the river, taking with him a girl she knew to be another member of the auxiliary. They had their theme now, and they were prepared to play it again and again, until they got what they were looking for. There was no question that Big Anthony had gone to Turman on Wednesday night, driving the gang's truck, and most likely in the company of Midge and another of the gang members. All they were trying to find out was *where* he had gone in Turman.

"This girl Midge," Carella said, introducing the second chorus of the same opera, and suddenly the woman in the kitchen said, "Eleanor?"

"Yes, Grandma?"

"Come make me some tea, Eleanor."

"Yes, Grandma," she said, and rose swiftly and left the room.

Carella looked at Kling and sighed. Kling shook his head wearily because he knew exactly what Carella was thinking. They'd been *that* close, and now maybe they would lose her.

The girl was in the kitchen for perhaps five minutes. When she came back, she sat again in the easy chair, folded her hands in her lap, and said, "Well, I'm sorry I can't help you, but I don't know where Big is, and I don't know anybody named Midge." She was back to the litany, repeating whatever Randy had told her on the telephone.

"Ever been to Turman?" Kling asked. They weren't about to let her slip away. If they were forced to, they would baldly state that her boy friend had been caught with Midge *in flagrante delicto,* in the middle of Turman's Main Street, during the height of last night's rush hour.

"Turman?"

"Turman, Turman," Carella said, his tone sharper,

"right across the Hamilton Bridge. Now don't tell us you don't know where Turman is."

Ellie shrank back from the harshness of his voice. "Yes, I know where Turman is."

"Have you ever been there?"

"I . . . don't remember."

That meant she'd been there. The rest would all be downhill. But instead of relaxing, their manner got tougher, their voices more demanding, their very postures more rigid and unrelenting.

"You'd *better* remember," Kling said.

"And *fast*," Carella said.

"If I can't remember, I can't remember," Ellie said. Her blue eyes were beginning to swim with tears.

"Have you ever been to Turman, yes or no?" Carella snapped.

"Yes, all right, yes. I think I was there. But only once."

"When?"

"I don't remember."

"Now you listen to me, Ellie," Carella said, and pointed his finger at her. "You're going to find yourself in a whole lot of trouble if you don't start telling us the truth."

"We're wasting time," Kling said in apparent disgust. "Let's take her to the station house."

"No, wait a minute, what for?" Ellie said. Her tearfilled eyes were wide with panic now.

"When did you go to Turman?"

"Just before Christmas."

"Where?"

"I don't re—"

"*Where,* damn it!" Carella shouted.

"It's a big town. I don't remember."

"It's a small town, and you *do* remember!"

"What's the matter, Eleanor?" the woman in the kitchen asked.

"Where?" Carella said again.

"Is something wrong, Eleanor?" the woman asked. "What's that shouting?"

Kling rose abruptly from the sofa. "Your grandmother's going to have to post bail for you," he lied. "Come on, get your coat."

"No, wait, I . . ."

"Yes?" Carella said.

"What have I *done?*" Ellie asked plaintively. "I mean, what is it I've *done?*"

"You're withholding evidence," Kling said. "Let's go." He reached for the handcuffs on his belt. That's what did it. He would remember always that reaching for the handcuffs was what caused the girl to crack. He would remember the trick, and use it again and again in the future.

"All right, I went to a house there," Ellie said softly, and lowered her head, and stared at her feet.

"What house?" Carella said quickly.

"Big's aunt has a house in Turman."

"Where? What street?"

"I don't know."

"Damn it . . ." Kling started.

"I *really* don't know, I swear to God! It's a yellow house with white shutters, and there's a fig tree in the front yard. It was covered with tarpaper when we were there in December. I don't know the street. I was only there that once. I swear to God, I don't know the street!"

"What's his aunt's name?"

"Martha Walsh."

"Where does she live?"

"Around the corner. On Phillips Avenue."

"Thank you," Carella said.

"Eleanor?" the woman in the kitchen asked. "Are you all right?"

"I'm all right," Ellie said without conviction.

DETECTIVE MEYER MEYER was having his problems with public relations.

Montgomery Pierce-Hoyt was on the telephone again, and he wanted to know whether or not the lieutenant had given Meyer permission to discuss the relationship of television to acts of violence.

"Yes, he's given me permission," Meyer said. "Provided it's clearly understood that whatever I say is only my own personal opinion, and isn't in any way presented as the official view of the department."

"Oh, yes, certainly," Pierce-Hoyt said. "When can I come up there?"

"I was just leaving the office," Meyer said.

"When will you be back?"

"I have a speaking engagement, and then I'm going straight home."

"A speaking engagement?" Pierce-Hoyt asked. "What kind of speaking engagement?"

"I'm talking at a women's college."

"What about?"

"Rape. How to prevent it."

"That sounds intriguing," Pierce-Hoyt said.

"Yes, it's very intriguing," Meyer said dryly.

"Mind if I come along?"

"I'm leaving right this minute."

"I'll meet you there. I'd like to hear your talk. Might provide some interesting sidelights for the piece. Which college is it?"

"Amberson."

"What time are you speaking?"

"Three o'clock," Meyer said, and couldn't resist adding, "if I can get off the phone."

"I'll be there. How will I know you?"

"I'll be the only one standing on the platform behind a lectern and talking about rape."

"See you," Pierce-Hoyt said cheerfully, and hung up.

Meyer did not like Pierce-Hoyt. He had not even met him, and already he didn't like him. He also didn't like having to go all the way downtown and crosstown on a Saturday to give a talk on rape-prevention to a crowd of young girls who were probably living in dormitories with men students from nearby colleges and screwing their brains out. When his daughter Susie got old enough, he would say No. No, you may *not* take a boy as a college roommate. No, you may *not* bring a boy home to this house and sleep in the same bedroom with him. Yes, I *am* an old-fashioned man, that's right. If this were Poland, where my grandfather came from, and if we went to the village rabbi and asked, "Rov, is it fitting that my only daughter should sleep with a person before she's married?," the rabbi would shake his head and stroke his beard, and answer, "Nowhere is it written that such an act should be condoned." The answer is No, Susie. No, no, no.

He went to the coat rack, and was putting on his coat when the telephone rang. Cotton Hawes and Hal Willis were supposed to be working the shift with him, but he hadn't seen hide nor hair of either of them since lunchtime. Muttering, he picked up the receiver.

"87th Squad, Detective Meyer," he said.

"Meyer, this is Grundy here in Turman. Is Carella around?"

"Grundy?" Meyer said. "Who's Grundy?"

"Detective Grundy, Turman Police."

"Hello, Grundy, how are you?"

"Fine. Is Carella there?"

"Not at the moment. Anything I can do for you?"

"Yeah. Tell him we located the truck. Green sixty-four Chevy, bearing an Isola plate, 74J-8309, registered to one Randall M. Nesbitt, address 1104 Dooley in Riverhead. Back of the truck scrubbed clean, not a stain of any kind on it. We're checking the steering wheel, gearshift, everything else inside and out for latents, but our guess is we won't find a thing."

"Where'd you . . . ?"

"I was coming to that," Grundy said. "There's a pond about six miles from where we found the girl's body. Truck was half submerged there. Guess they thought it was deeper than it actually is."

"What time . . . ?"

"Found it a little after noon. Mailman driving by spotted the back of it sticking out of the water."

"Anything else?"

"That's it. Will you tell Carella?"

"Sure thing."

"If he's got any questions, I'll be here till about six tonight."

"I'll leave the message."

"Thanks," Grundy said, and hung up.

Meyer wrote out the note for Carella, glanced at the wall clock, and wondered if the lieutenant had chosen him for this lecture only because he was bald, and therefore presumably looked fatherly, and therefore capable of inspiring confidence in clean-scrubbed college girls. Meyer did not think he looked fatherly. Meyer thought he looked quite handsome and dashing—which he would *have* to be if he was to get to Amberson by three o'clock. He was buttoning his coat and going through the gate in the railing, when he heard Kling and Carella coming up the iron-runged steps to the second floor. They came into the corridor just as he reached the stairway. "Call from Turman," he said. "They found the truck. Note's on your desk." Racing down the steps, he shouted over his shoulder, "I'll be going home straight from the college. See you Monday."

"*What* college?" Carella shouted after him. "What are you talking about?"

But Meyer was gone.

Carella read the note on his desk, and called Grundy

back at once. It was now almost two-thirty, and there wasn't a moment to lose. A state trooper answered the telephone, and then switched Carella over to Grundy's office.

"Yeah?" Grundy said.

"I got your message. We've been doing some work on this end, talking to the suspect's girl friend, and later his aunt. We've got a house we want you to check out."

"Here in Turman?"

"Right. Here's the address, have you got a pencil?"

"Shoot," Grundy said.

"304 West Scovil Lane. Ring a bell?"

"I know the area. Whose house is it?"

"Belongs to the suspect's aunt, woman named Martha Walsh. She told us she keeps it closed during the winter, but the suspect has a key."

"You still haven't told me *his* name," Grundy said.

"Big Anthony Sutherland."

"That would be 'Pig,' huh? And the second kid?"

"No help."

"I'm on my way," Grundy said.

WHILE Meyer Meyer told an assorted collection of not-so-virginal college girls that a rapist was a seriously disturbed individual who was incapable of enjoying a normal sex relationship with a woman, Detective Al Grundy drove along tree-shaded Scovil Lane, and located a yellow house with white shutters bearing the number 304 on the mailbox outside. And while Meyer told his audience that a rapist *expects* his victim to be terrified, and that this terror-reaction adds to his own excitement, Grundy went up the front walk past the tarpaper-covered fig tree, and knocked on the front door and got no answer, and forced the lock.

"Now some of you may feel that rape is not such a terrible thing. It is penetration by force, true, it is a violation of your body, true—but if you submit to this violation, perhaps you will not be hurt. Perhaps. But remember that part of the psychological interplay that makes rape appealing and exciting to this man is the very taking-by-force aspect of what he's doing. And where there is force involved, there is the attendant danger of being severely beaten or even killed."

There was a sleeping bag on the floor of the living room, and bedclothes on the living-room couch. An empty pizza carton and two empty cans of beer were on the floor. An ashtray brimming with butts rested on the end table alongside the couch. Grundy sniffed the butts on the off chance they might be marijuana roaches. They were not. He went into the kitchen.

"I don't want you to become neurotic about rape, I don't want you to start screaming if a panhandler taps you on the shoulder. He may only want a quarter for a drink, and you'll start screaming, and he'll try to shut you up, and the next thing you know he's broken your neck. That's as bad as being assaulted by a *real* rapist. I do want to frighten you a bit, however, and the first thing I want to frighten you about is hitchhiking. If you'd like to get raped, the best way to accomplish your goal is to go outside and start hitchhiking. I can't guarantee that if you hitch a ride tonight, you'll positively be raped. But I *can* guarantee that if you hitch from the same spot at the same time each night, someone will try to rape you. It might take a week, it might take longer. But someone will try. And it will have nothing whatever to do with how you look. You can be standing on that corner wearing a potato sack, with your hair in curlers, and a fever sore on your lip, and that won't discourage the rapist. He is a sick man; you are presumably a healthy individual. Don't, for God's sake, foolishly place yourself in hazardous or vulnerable situations."

There were two six-packs of beer in the refrigerator, a carton of milk, some cold cuts, and a package of sliced bread with half the loaf gone. Used paper plates were on the kitchen table, and the trash can was full of empty cans—baked beans, soup, vegetables, hash. Cups, silverware, soup plates, and knives were piled in the sink, unwashed. Grundy went into the bedroom.

"Like in the song from *The Fantasticks,* there are many different kinds of rape. If you're out on a date with a man you know, and you're necking in his automobile, and he decides to take you by force, against your wishes, that's *rape*—even if you've known him since he was six years old. In a situation like that, I would advise that you stop necking for a moment, stick your finger down your throat, and vomit into his lap. The more serious rape, if rapes can be classified as to seriousness, is the one that can lead to bodily injury or death. A man jumps out at you, he threatens you at knife point. Don't begin telling him what a disgusting animal he is, don't start cutting him down to size, because he may decide to cut *you* down to size—literally. He is emotionally unstable, he does not need his ego further bruised. I've known victims who have talked themselves out of being raped by treating their attacker with human kindness, understanding, sympathy, and humility. This doesn't always work, but it may at least buy you some time until either help comes or you can effect an escape. One girl bought time by telling the rapist she *knew* he'd been following her, and thought she was the luckiest girl alive, because here she was just a plain, dumpy little thing, and he was such a big handsome man. She put her arms around his neck and got very affectionate—something totally unexpected by the rapist—and he lost his erection and was momentarily incapable of performing. By the time he got back to the business at hand, which was taking this girl by *force,* don't forget that, some people wandered up the street, and the girl was saved from attack.

"But let's suppose a man begins hitting you the moment he drags you into the bushes. Your natural reaction, even if you plan *not* to resist, even if you plan to go limp—which may cause the same thing to happen to *him*—is to turn your head away from the blows, or bring up your hands to protect your face, or in some way involuntarily show resistance or fear, which will only provoke him more. Let's say nothing you've said or done has worked, you are on the ground, he is still striking you, he is going to rape you. The question now is whether you want to be raped, and maybe killed, or whether you want to hurt this man. Only you can decide that. If you choose not to be a victim, I can tell you how to hurt him, and how to get away from him."

The bedclothes were rumpled, the sheets were stained with blood. A leather-thonged cat-o'-nine-tails was on the floor near the footboard. The window was wide open. Grundy went to the window and looked out. The ground was some four feet below the sill. He carefully tented his handkerchief over the leather-wrapped handle of the whip, and then tagged it for identification and subsequent transmittal to the police lab in nearby Allenby. A girl's handbag was resting on the seat of a straight-backed chair near the bed. Grundy opened the bag.

"Remember that the unexpected is the best approach. You are flat on your back, and this man is about to rape you. Instead of trying to twist away, instead of trying to shove him off you, begin to fondle him. That's right. Fondle the man. Fondle his genitals. And then drop your hand to his testicles and squeeze. Squeeze as hard as you can. You are going to hurt this man, but you are also going to end the rape that very minute. You may wonder whether he will be able to chase you afterwards, perhaps hit you harder than he did before, perhaps even kill you. I can guarantee that you can run clear to California and back, and that man will still be lying on the ground incapable of move-ment. This is one way of stopping a rape, if you do not choose to become a victim. There is another way, and I suspect your reaction to it will be 'I'd rather get raped.' That, of course, is up to you. I can only offer you options."

The girl's handbag contained three lipsticks, a package of Kleenex, two sticks of chewing gum, four subway tokens, three dollar bills, forty cents in change, and a card showing that she was a member of the Student Organization of Whitman High School in Riverhead. The name on the card identified her as Margaret McNally. There was nothing in the house or on the grounds outside that in any way identified the two boys who presumably had killed her.

"Again, do the unexpected," Meyer said. "Put your hands gently on the rapist's face, palms against his temples, cradle his face, murmur words of endearment, allow him to think you're going along with his plans. Your thumbs will be close to his eyes. If you have in yourself the courage to push your thumbs into a hard-boiled egg, then you can also push them into this man's eyes. You will put out his eyes, you will blind him. But you will not be raped. There is never a moment, during a rape in progress, I can guarantee this, when you will not have the opportunity to fondle the man's genitals or to put your hands on his face. These are his vulnerable areas, and if you behave unexpectedly and do not seem to be preparing an attack, he will not suspect what is coming until it is too late. Squeezing his testicles will incapacitate him, but may not permanently injure him. Putting out his eyes is a drastic measure, and you may feel with some justification that doing this is worse than what the rapist is trying to do to you—that the means of preventing the rape are worse than the crime itself. The choice is yours."

Meyer wiped his brow with his handkerchief, and then asked, "Are there any questions?"

7

THE way them Scarlet niggers got hold of Big Anthony and Jo-Jo was pure accident, and it was what started all the later trouble. I wouldn't be up here now, if it wasn't for what happened yesterday.

I had got a call late Thursday night, it must've been three or four o'clock in the morning, it got me out of bed. My people know that I'm available at all hours of the day and night, that's what being president means. You serve the people. I am always cheerful and courteous on the telephone, no matter what time it is. The phone in my house is in the kitchen, and I went out there in my undershorts, and it was very cold, they cut off the heat in the building at about eleven o'clock each night, that's to discourage the rats from coming out of their nice warm hiding places. I'm making a joke, but it's true there's no heat from eleven at night to maybe seven or eight in the morning, those cheap landlords. Anyway, I'm standing there freezing in my underwear, and Big Anthony tells me he's calling from a phone booth outside a diner on Route 14 in Turman and that he had to take very severe measures with Midge. That's a code thing we have in the clique, the "severe measures." It means, you know, that he had to like kill her.

I remained very calm, I am always calm. I told Big he had probably done the right thing, if in his judgment the thing had to be done, and I asked him if there had been any witnesses, and he said No, he did not think so. I told him in that case he should go back to his aunt's house and just keep cool, stay out of the city, we would keep close watch on the situation and see what developed. That was on Thursday night—well, really it was Friday morning already. On Saturday you guys came around and talked to me in the ice cream parlor, with your phony story about first a hold-up of a gas station and later you changed it to wanting Midge for a mugging, all of which I knew was absolute bullhenge. You guys thought you were being so clever, but there's nothing gets by me. Actually, you were doing me a favor. Because you were letting me know the truck was hot, and that you were looking for Big Anthony in connection with Midge's murder. That's all you accomplished by your little visit. I gave you the name of Big's girl because I couldn't see no harm in your going to see her, especially since I planned to phone her the minute you left. Which I done, of course, and warned her to keep her mouth shut, to tell you she didn't know where Big was, and she never heard of nobody named Midge. The minute I hung up, I called Big at his aunt's house in Turman, and told him to get rid of the truck, as it was hot. I also told him to get out of Turman and get back here to the city, because I knew all the heat would be *there,* you dig, and nobody would think of looking for him back *here.* That was smart thinking.

I'm always on my feet and looking how to outfox the other guy.

So it gets to be Sunday, yesterday, and no word from Big. At first I thought he was playing it extremely cool, that he had got back to the city with Jo-Jo, and the two of them were holed up someplace and didn't want to risk even making a phone call, because like who can tell what's bugged and what isn't these days? The way I figure it, if *we* can put in a bug, why then, anybody in the whole United States can put one in. What's to stop them? And maybe Big was thinking the same way, and was afraid to call. I was watching the football game on television, just me and Toy. My mother was across the street, visiting her sister. My old man was out drinking, as usual. He's on welfare, and he's got tuberculosis, but that don't stop him from putting away the sauce. He can't pass a bar without marching in there and drinking himself into a stupor. He's very proud of me because he knows I'm president of an important clique. I respect him and honor him except for the drinking. I can't abide anything done to excess. He is foolish to drink so much, and to lose control of himself. Control is the important thing. To be in control all the time is my watchword. Anyway, I was glad he was out of the house because it gave me some time to relax with Toy and to watch the football. The game was a very exciting one, and it took my mind off why Big hadn't called yet. I didn't want to think that something had happened to him, that maybe he had been picked up by the Turman fuzz before he'd made it back to the city.

The telephone rang about three o'clock in the afternoon, just at a very exciting play in the game. I went out in the kitchen to answer it, hoping it would be Big. Instead, it was Mighty Man, the war counselor of the Scarlets.

Hello, he says, how's every little thing up there on Dooley Avenue?

Just fine, I tell him, to what do I owe the honor of this call?

We got two of your boys, he says.

What boys? I ask him. What are you talking about?

Well, he tells me what he's talking about. What he's talking about is that by the craziest freak accident, Big and Jo-Jo stumbled into a party of Scarlets and they took them both prisoner. Now this is the way it happened. The Scarlets will tell you all kinds of bullhenge about how Big and Jo-Jo had defected, but that ain't the truth. It was accident, pure and simple, they are both loyal men.

The minute they ditched the truck, Big and Jo-Jo figured if the truck was hot, then their clique jackets were hot, too, because of what's painted on the back— our symbol, you know? So they took off the jackets, and rolled them up, and started hitchhiking in just their sweaters. I mean, man, Saturday was a cold mother of a day, am I right? They hiked for maybe two hours before somebody picked them up, and he dropped them off just near the bridge, and they walked over and then took the subway up to Riverhead. It was when they got off the subway on Hitchcock that they ran into trouble.

The trouble had to do with cops, and it was just a crazy kind of coincidence thing, because what happened was that a pack of dogs was attacking this little kid in the street, and there must've been a thousand cops' cars there trying to get the dogs off her—Big told me later he never seen so many cops in his life. And cops were running from all over the neighborhood, too, to help out with this wild-dog situation; somebody must've called in an assist-patrolman or something, the whole area was swarming with fuzz. So Big figured the next thing was one of the cops would spot him, maybe they had a description of him, and he'd be languishing downtown in Calcutta, that nice little jail you have, and so he done what I would have done under similar circumstances. He got back on the train and rode it to the next stop.

The next spot happened to be Gateside Avenue, which is where the Scarlets have their clubhouse. Big knows where the clubhouse is, and he had no intention of going any place near it. Him and Jo-Jo was going to circle Scarlet territory and head back downtown, hoping the fuzz would be gone by the time they got there. But they were both very hungry by now, this was maybe like four o'clock in the afternoon, it was already starting to get dark. They hadn't eaten anything since breakfast that morning because the minute I called them they left the house and ditched the truck and started for the city. That must've been about, I don't know, what time did you guys find me in the ice cream parlor? Eleven-thirty, something like that? Anyway, it was now the afternoon, and they were hungry, so they stopped in this pizzeria and ordered a large pie with sausage, and they were eating it when five big black guys came in the place, and they're all wearing those red jackets with the white sleeves, they're all Scarlet Avengers.

There was no way for Big and Jo-Jo to get out of the place in time. They were eating pizza in one of the booths there, and next thing you know the booth is surrounded, and Big and Jo-Jo aren't carrying because they're afraid they might get picked up and they don't want no weapons on them if that happens, and all the niggers are armed. One of them shows Big this .45 he's got under his coat, and he tells Big to get out of the booth nice and easy and come along with him or he's going to blow his brains out all over the pizza.

Big and Jo-Jo are brave men, they will never back out of a fight. But the odds here were just too much, so they went along with the Scarlets, and that was what started the whole prisoner issue. What Mighty Man was telling me on the phone was that he had Big and Jo-Jo in his custody, at a place we would never find, and that he would not release them until we negotiated a peace that was satisfactory to his clique. He also mentioned that he was showing the Rebs a great deal of consideration by not executing Big and Jo-Jo on the spot, since they were members of a clique responsible for killing their president and his wife and kid. How do you like *that* reasoning? I had ordered last week's Sunday night hit because I was trying to speed up peaceful negotiations, so now Mighty Man was telling me he considered members of my clique to be criminals! You see how devious that kind of thinking is? You go along with that kind of thinking, and then anything you do to protect yourself, or your honor, or your sincere efforts to bring some peace to this neighborhood becomes like you're doing something *bad* instead of something *good*. Man, I wasn't buying Mighty Man's line for a minute, I can tell you that. I know what's right, and it ain't right to pick up two guys who are eating pizza and minding their own business, and then holding them prisoner, and using them to get terms you wouldn't otherwise get.

So I told Mighty Man there would be no further negotiations till Big and Jo-Jo were released, and Mighty Man says there will be no release until we negotiate further. He also says What about killing Lewis and his wife and his kid, and I tell him I don't know anything about who killed any of those people, but I certainly will join him in finding the criminals once he releases the prisoners he is holding and we can negotiate a just peace. I also tell him that if he harms either Big or Jo-Jo, he had better watch his ass. I never curse, as I told you, but I was dealing here with a disgusting animal, and I had to talk to him in his own language. I made it even more perfectly clear to him. I told him that if anything happened to Big or Jo-Jo, he had better plan on spending the rest of his life in Fort Knox, because that would be the only place we couldn't get to him. And I told him he better have both of them back to us by midnight that night, which was Sunday, or on Monday he would begin to think that what had happened to his president was only playing jacks with little girls.

Mighty Man told me to go fuck myself.

Those were his exact words.

I'm using them now only to prove to you what kind of animals the Scarlets are, and what we were dealing with.

Midnight came and went, and still no Big or Jo-Jo. I called a meeting of the council and told them what I planned to do. Johnny refused to go along with it. He did not know yet that Midge was dead, but he refused to go along with the plan because he said he was tired of all the bloodshed and killing. He said he would rather quit the clique than get involved in any more killing. I explained to him and to the council that this wasn't killing human beings, this was killing disgusting animals, this was killing the *enemy*. And don't forget, I told him, that Big and Jo-Jo were right this minute going through God only knew what kind of ordeal—and Johnny interrupted and said What are they doing back here in the city? Where's Midge?

I told him there'd been a change of plans, that Midge was all right, and not to get me off the subject. The point was that Big and Jo-Jo were prisoners, and we were not going to sacrifice them to the enemy, and we were also not going to let up on the enemy as long as they were holding people of ours. I also told Johnny that there was no such *thing* as quitting the clique, that if he refused to go up against the Scarlets tomorrow night, why then, I would consider him a deserter and he might just as well move out of the country because he could never so much as set foot on Rebel turf again without having to pay the full penalty. There were too many guys in the clique who were willing to sacrifice even their lives for the good of us all, too many guys like Big and Jo-Jo who were right that minute in the hands of the enemy undergoing a tremendous ordeal so we could have a just and lasting peace, for me to look upon any deserter with kindness. If he expected to walk away from a fight, and then get amnesty from me, he had another think coming.

So Johnny said if he had to move to China, he would do it, but he wasn't going to kill nobody tomorrow night. So I told him to get out.

Where's Midge? he asked me again.

I told him that was none of his business, since he was a traitor to this clique and no longer a member of it with any rights.

He said he would find her, and then he left.

And that was when I told the council that severe measures seemed necessary and I ordered The Bullet and Chingo to go after Johnny and make sure he did not cause any further trouble for us.

CHARLIE BROUGHAN'S squad at the 101st caught the squeal. Broughan himself was on duty, and he went out at four in the morning, and talked to the r.m.p. men, and then walked into the empty lot where the body of the boy lay huddled against the fence. It was a bitter-cold night. Clothes stiff with frost hung on clotheslines stretched from a pole at one corner of the lot to various windows on the rear wall of the tenement behind the fence. The boy was wearing only trousers, socks, and a shirt. Two bullet holes were in the back of his head. He had either been shoeless when someone murdered him, or else his shoes had been stolen after he'd been killed. Broughan had been a cop for a long time, and he knew that killing someone for his shoes was not an impossibility in this part of the city. On the ground near the body he found two brass buttons with thread still clinging to them, and he assumed they had been torn loose from an article of clothing, probably some sort of jacket worn over the shirt. He bagged and tagged the buttons for transmittal to the lab.

A pack of wild dogs came into the lot while Broughan was working there. He did not fool around with them. He drew his pistol and killed first a German shepherd and then a huge brown-and-white-spotted mongrel. The four other dogs in the pack ran out of the lot, and Broughan got back to work looking for footprints, weapons, dropped personal articles, anything that would provide a start. When the medical examiner got through with the body, he went through the boy's pockets. He was not carrying any identification—*another* one, Broughan thought. He had a hunch at that point, and he asked the photographer to take a Polaroid of the boy's face, and he carried that back with him to the squadroom.

There were 2,117 photographs in Broughan's files on the street gangs of Riverhead. He had looked through 428 of them when he came across the one that matched the Polaroid shot of the murder victim. The back of the picture gave the boy's name as Jonathan

Quince, and his address as 782 Waverly. The boy had been an affiliate of a gang known as the Yankee Rebels.

Broughan looked at the wall clock.

It was 5:20 A.M.

He called the squadroom of the 87th, and Detective Bob O'Brien answered the phone. Broughan identified himself, and then said, "I got something that might interest Carella. Is he on?"

"Be in at about eight," O'Brien said.

"Would you ask him to call me the minute he gets in?"

"Right."

"Thanks."

Broughan hung up, debated calling Carella at home, and decided he'd let him sleep. This would wait a few hours.

He hoped.

JONATHAN QUINCE'S mother was a woman in her forties—squat, amply bosomed, blue-eyed, graying. At eight-thirty that Monday morning, January 14, when Carella and Kling arrived, she was dressed and ready to leave for work downtown in the garment center. They identified themselves and were let into the apartment. Mrs. Quince told them she hoped they'd make this fast, because it took twenty minutes to get to work by subway and she still hadn't had breakfast. She also hoped they wouldn't mind if she drank her coffee while they told her what the trouble was. She did not ask them if they'd care for a cup. Her son had been a member of a street gang, and they knew she'd had policemen up here before; her cordiality was somewhat forced, to say the least.

"Mrs. Quince," Carella said, "I'm sorry to have to be the one to bring you bad news, but . . ."

"Johnny," she said immediately and flatly, the name catching somewhere at the back of her throat.

"Yes."

"How bad is he hurt?"

"He's dead," Carella said.

"No."

Neither of the cops said anything.

"No," Mrs. Quince said again.

"I'm sorry," Carella said.

"How?"

"Someone shot him."

"Who?"

"We don't know."

"Those gangs," she said, and shook her head. A glazed look had come over her eyes, her entire face looked suddenly numbed. "I told him."

"Mrs. Quince, do you know a girl named Margaret McNally?"

"Midge? Yes. Why? Did she have something to do with this? Was it a fight over her?"

"No, ma'am. She was killed on Thursday night, and we under—"

"Oh my God," Mrs. Quince said. "Oh my God, what's happening?"

"We understand she was your son's girl friend."

Mrs. Quince did not answer. She was staring into

her coffee cup as though hoping to find denial there.

"Mrs. Quince?"

"Yes," she said blankly. "She was his girl friend. Yes."

"The possibility exists, Mrs. Quince, that their deaths are related. We're not quite sure what's going on yet, but . . ."

"Where is he?" she asked suddenly.

"Your son? At the morgue. Washington Hospital."

"Are you sure it's him?"

"Yes, we're relatively certain. Detective Broughan, whose case this is—"

"What do you mean? Isn't this *your* case?"

"Not officially. The detective who answers the complaint is normally assigned to the case."

"Then how do you know it's Johnny?"

"Because Detective Broughan had a picture taken, and it matches a—"

"Pictures can lie."

"—a picture in his files," Carella concluded. "We don't think there's been a mistake, Mrs. Quince. I'm sorry."

"I want to go to the morgue," she said. "I want to make sure. I want to see for myself."

"Of course."

"I knew this would happen," she said. "Sooner or later, I knew it would happen."

"What makes you say that?"

"From the time of the abortion, I knew this would happen."

"What abortion? Can you tell us what you mean?"

"When Midge wanted to have the abortion, and they said no."

"Who said no?"

"Johnny's gang. The boys in his gang. They said no, she couldn't have one. The kids came to me, they said they wanted to get married because the gang said Midge couldn't have the abortion. I refused. Midge was only fifteen, Johnny was seventeen at the time. How can you let two kids get married when they're so young? I told them I agreed with . . . whatever his name is . . . the one with the fake smile, the one who's president. Put the baby up for adoption. I made a mistake. The kids never got over it. Both of them. And Johnny began having trouble with the gang from the minute Midge had the baby and put it up for adoption. I thought I was doing the right thing. They were such kids. How can you let two *children* get married. They didn't know, it's not easy, my own marriage . . . they didn't know. I was trying to help them. I made a mistake. I should have given them my blessings and told them to go ahead. Then maybe this wouldn't have happened. Maybe he'd have broken with the gang once and for all, and this wouldn't have happened." She seemed to remember something terribly significant, and said with an air of surprise, "Johnny's birthday was two weeks ago. He was just eighteen. I want to go to the hospital. I want to make sure it's him. I have to make sure. Do you see? Do you understand?"

"Yes, Mrs. Quince."

"Because I have to make sure."

"Mrs. Quince, I know you'd like us to catch whoever killed your son, and maybe you can help us do that."

"Yes," she said. Her voice was toneless. She seemed not to be listening.

"I'm going to tell you what we already know, and also what we believe. We know that Midge McNally was found dead in the woods off Highway 14 in Turman, across the river, early Friday morning. An eyewitness at the scene saw two boys wearing Yankee Rebel gang jackets, as well as a truck bearing the Yankee Rebel insignia on its door panels. We've since found the truck, abandoned, and we've also found the house in which we believe Midge was being held captive. It belongs to a woman named Martha Walsh, who's the aunt of a Yankee Rebel named Big Anthony."

"Yes," Mrs. Quince said.

"We have very good reason to believe that Big Anthony and another boy took Midge to Turman last Wednesday night, and then for some reason killed her. We don't know why yet. Nor have we yet located Big Anthony."

"Do you think he killed my son?"

"We don't know. Once we find him, we'll be able to ask him some questions. We've got enough right now to make an arrest. Which is where we can use your help."

"What help?" she asked.

"In finding him. In finding Big Anthony."

"How can I help you?"

"Was there any place . . . did Johnny ever mention any place that members of his gang would go to if they needed . . . well, if they needed to be out of sight for a while?"

"What do you mean?"

"To hide."

"Hide?"

"From the police. Was there such a place, here in the city, that they could go to? Other than the clubhouse on Hitchcock and Dooley? A place the police might not know about?"

"I don't know of any such place here in the city."

"Detective Broughan's files indicate that Johnny'd been in trouble with the law on several occasions . . ."

"Yes," she said, and nodded.

"We're particularly interested in June of last year, when the 101st Squad couldn't locate your son for six days. He finally walked into the station house and said he didn't know they'd been looking for him, but there he was, and what did they want to know. Apparently he'd been hiding someplace till a suitable alibi could be concocted for him. Do you remember that incident, Mrs. Quince?"

"No."

"It involved a shooting."

"No, I don't remember."

"Last June. The latter part of the month."

"No."

"Would you remember whether or not Johnny was gone from the apartment any time last June?"

"No."

"You *do* remember the police coming here to ask for him. Detective Broughan? Of the 101st Squad?"

"Yes, I remember that. But I'm not here all the time, you see."

"But you *were* here when Detective Broughan came around asking for Johnny. That was in June, Mrs. Quince."

"Yes, I was here. But only because I'd come back for something, I forget what. I think I'd taken the wrong shoes, I think that was it. Black shoes, I think, when I needed my blue ones. Yes, that was it. I'm not here a lot of the time, you see."

"Where are you?" Kling asked.

"I stay with a friend of mine. My husband and I are separated, you see."

"Were you staying with your friend in June? When Johnny was missing for six days?"

"I suppose so, I really don't remember. I'm not here too often. I don't like this building. I don't like the people in this building. A lot of spics are beginning to move in. I stay with my friend a lot of the time. Johnny's a big boy, you see, he can take care of himself." She hesitated, realizing what she had just said. "I . . . I always thought he could take care of himself," she said. "I couldn't be expected to . . . I couldn't be expected to watch over him every minute. He was eighteen years old. When I was eighteen, I was already married."

"Do you have any other children, Mrs. Quince?" Kling asked.

"I *had* another son. He was killed in Vietnam."

"I'm sorry."

"Yes," Mrs. Quince said, and nodded. "My husband left in 1965, I don't think he even knows our oldest boy got killed in the war. I wonder if he'll ever find out they're *both* dead now. Or if he'll even care. I heard he was living in Seattle. Somebody said they saw him in Seattle, I forget who. Somebody. They said he seemed very happy." Mrs. Quince nodded again. "It's difficult raising two boys alone, you know. A man should be around to . . . to . . . I don't know," she said, and shrugged. "It's difficult. I did my best. I tried to do the right thing. When Roger wanted to enlist, I said no, but he went anyway. And when I found out Johnny was running around with a gang, I tried to talk to him, but . . . you know . . . it's very difficult when there isn't a man in the house. They just tell you to go to hell, you know? You're their mother, but they say Go to hell, and then they do what they want to do. Johnny was no saint, he'd been in trouble with the law since he was twelve. The time he shot that other boy was the worst, I suppose . . ."

"Was that last June, Mrs. Quince?"

"Yes. The time you were talking about. He shot a boy who belonged to another gang, I forget the name of the gang, they have such dumb names, it's all so dumb."

"Would it have been the Death's Heads?"

"I don't know. I don't remember."

"When Detective Broughan came around looking for Johnny . . . did you know at the time that he'd shot someone?"

"Yes."

"But you didn't tell that to Detective Broughan?"

"No."

"Do you know what happened to that boy your son shot, Mrs. Quince?"

"Yes. He died in Washington Hospital."

"Yes," Carella said.

"Yes, I know." She lifted her chin, her eyes met Carella's. "What did you want me to do, mister? Turn him in? He was my son. I'd lost one the November before, I wasn't about to lose another one. Not that it matters now. You live around here, it catches up. It *has* to catch up." She lowered her eyes again. "I don't know any rich men's sons who got killed in that war over there, do you? And I don't know any rich men's sons who get killed in the street in the middle of the night. If there's a God, mister, he doesn't know about poor people."

"Mrs. Quince," Carella said, "when Detective Broughan was looking for your son last June, did you know where he was hiding?"

"Yes," she said. "I knew."

"Where?" Carella asked, and leaned forward.

"It won't help you," Mrs. Quince said. "He was at that house in Turman."

At four o'clock that afternoon, precisely one week and twelve hours after the six bodies had been found in the telephone-company ditch, Carella got a phone call from Phyllis Kingsley, sister of the bearded white man who'd spent time with Eduardo and Constantina

Portoles on the night all three of them were murdered. Phyllis told him she had been contacted by a girl named Lisa Knowles, who had flown in from California the moment she'd learned of Andrew Kingsley's death. The girl wanted to talk to the police. She was staying at the Farragut Hotel in midtown Isola.

Carella thanked Phyllis, hung up for just an instant, and then placed a call to the Farragut.

8

E did not get downtown until a little after five o'clock.

Night had descended on the city, the street lamps were on, the homeward rush of office workers had already begun. He drove for two blocks, looking for a parking space, and finally had to put the car in a garage. He did not particularly enjoy this because he knew he wouldn't be reimbursed for the cost of the parking, no matter how many chits he put in. The streets were bleakly cold. Pedestrians went past him swiftly, heading for subway kiosks and bus stops, their heads ducked against the fierce wind, hands clutched into coat collars or stuffed into pockets. He looked up at the sky and hoped it would not snow. He did not like snow. Teddy had once talked him into trying skiing, and he had almost broken his leg the first time down, and had given up on skiing *and* on snow and *also* on cold weather that got into a man's bones and made him miserable all over. He thought of Midge

McNally lying in mud and leaves in the woods, her blouse stiff with blood. He thought of Johnny Quince, two bullets in the back of his head, shoeless, wearing only trousers and a shirt. And he thought of the six naked corpses lying in the telephone-company ditch. He hurried toward the hotel.

The Farragut was a fleabag catering to hookers, junkies, pushers, and pimps. If Carella had cared to make a few dozen arrests while he was on the premises, just so the trip downtown shouldn't be a total loss, he could have done so with ease. But this was not his precinct, and presumably there were cops here to protect the citizenry, uphold the morality, and continue the unceasing war against narcotics abuse; he would let *their* mothers worry. In the meantime, the preconceived opinion he formed of Lisa Knowles was not a very good one. What's a nice girl like you doing in a place like this? he asked himself, even before he met her.

As it turned out, Lisa Knowles *was* a nice girl. She just didn't have very much money, and she had taken a room at the Farragut only because it was the least expensive thing she could find. Lisa was the very picture of blooming, bursting, youthful California health. She looked nineteen, a barefooted, very tall girl—at least five-nine—with bright blue eyes sparkling against a suntanned face, blond hair cascading to the small of her back, long legs encased in blue jeans, firm breasts braless under a tight white cotton T-shirt. Greeting him at the door to her room, she immediately apologized for the dump she was living in, and then explained how short she was of cash. Carella followed her into the room, and she closed the door behind him. There was a bed in the room, and a single easy chair, and a standing floor lamp, and a cigarette-scarred dresser. Lisa sat cross-legged on the bed. Carella took the easy chair.

"I understand you want to talk to us," he said.

"Yes." She emphasized the single word with a curt nod of her blond head. She had big hands and big feet; she was a big girl all over. He could visualize her on a Malibu beach, wearing a bikini, riding a surfboard. He could also, and he was surprised by the unbidden image, visualize her in bed. He immediately got back to business.

"What about?" he said.

"Andrew Kingsley. I got a letter from him four days after he was killed. He'd written it last Saturday. I would have taken it to the California fuzz . . ." She smiled radiantly. "*Cops,* excuse me," she said. "Only I figured they'd just brush it off because it wasn't their case. Was I right?"

"Well, I don't know. The Los Angeles police are a pretty efficient bunch," Carella said, and returned the smile. "I'm sure they would have contacted us."

"How'd you know it was Los Angeles? And not San Francisco or San Diego or whatever?"

"Because Kingsley's sister told us he'd been doing work in Watts. That's Los Angeles," Carella said, and shrugged.

"Smart, smart," Lisa said, and tapped her temple with her forefinger. "Anyway, I raised the bread and came here personally. I didn't want to take a chance on the letter going astray, because I think it may help you find whoever killed him. Also, my folks are down in Miami, and a visit is long overdue, so I figured I'd kill two birds with one stone. Provided they send me the air fare. I'm afraid to give them the address of this dump, they might recognize it and call out the Marines. But I *have* to wire them because all I've got is about thirty cents to my name—that's an exaggeration, but really, I'm almost flat. If I don't get some financial help real soon, I'll have to join the hookers in this place." She smiled again. The image of Lisa Knowles as prostitute suddenly filled the small, shoddy, cheerless room. Lisa in garter belt and open-crotch panties, long blond hair spread on the pillow, Lisa being used and abused by drunken sailors and . . .

"How old are you?" Carella asked abruptly.

"Twenty-two. Why?" she said.

"Just wondered."

"Old enough," she said, "don't worry," and again she smiled her radiant smile, and Carella suddenly felt terribly uncomfortable and wanted to get out of there, and go home, and say to his wife, "Hey, guess what, honey? A beautiful twenty-two-year-old blonde was flirting with me today, what do you think of that, honey?" Except that Lisa Knowles wasn't flirting. Or was she? It was she, after all, who'd made the reference to prostitution. Why are you showing me all these dirty pictures, Doctor? Carella thought, and smiled.

"Yes?" she said.

"What?"

"Why are you smiling?"

"I just thought of something very funny," he said, and then became all business again. "Mind if I see the letter?"

"Oh, sure," she said, and got off the bed, and went across the room, long legs devouring the worn linoleum, backside round and firm in the tight blue jeans— Now *listen,* Carella told himself, and watched despite the self-admonition as she dug into the leather shoulder bag on the dresser top and came up with a red-and-blue-bordered air-mail envelope. She walked back to where he was sitting, and stopped just before the chair, her knees almost touching his. He took the envelope from her, adjusted the shade on the lamp for better illumination, and then removed the letter from the envelope and unfolded it. Lisa moved behind the chair so that she could read over his shoulder.

"See the date?" she said. "He was killed last Sunday, am I right? The letter was written on Saturday."

"Yes, that's right," Carella said, and began reading the letter:

Darling Golden Girl, how are you? I'm still here crashing with my sister, which is something of a drag, but I've finally made some contacts, and I think I'll be able to get started soon on the work I came east for.

"He used to call me Golden Girl," Lisa said.

"Mmm," Carella said.

"Because I'm a blonde."

"I see that."

147

He was about to say something more. He changed his mind, and started reading the rest of the letter:

Tomorrow night, I'll be going uptown to talk to the president of a gang that calls itself The Death's Heads. This is a Puerto Rican gang, and the leader is a fellow named Eduardo Portoles, who I met through Julio Cabrera. You remember him, he's the one who used to play piano at the Sunset Shrine, on the Strip. He's here now, playing Tuesdays and Fridays at a place downtown in The Quarter, barely eking out a living, but doing what he likes best—which is all that matters, am I right, Goldilocks?

He also called me Goldilocks," Lisa said.

"Because you're a blonde, I'll bet."

"How'd you guess?"

"Smart, smart," Carella said, and tapped his temple as she had done earlier.

"Listen, you don't happen to live here in the city, do you?" Lisa asked suddenly.

"Yes. Well, no, not downtown here. I live up in Riverhead. Why?"

"Just wondered," she said.

Anyway, Julio introduced me to this Portoles fellow who lives in the same neighborhood Julio grew up in, and that's how I got to know what the situation is up there. The situation, to put it mildly, stinks. In fact, my dear, it is putridly ripe for the likes of yours truly, Andrew Kingsley, to step in and try to make some progress before everybody kills everybody else. Lisa, the gangs up there are currently engaged in what amounts to full-scale warfare, and unless somebody can show them a peaceful way to settle their differences, a lot of innocent people are going to suffer. I say this with the knowledge that only two weeks ago, a mother wheeling her baby in the park was acci-

"Because I thought if I have to stay in this hotel one more night, I'll go out of my mind," Lisa said. "I was coming up the stairs today, and I saw a guy shooting up right on the second-floor landing. I mean, can you imagine that? He's got the rubber tied around his arm, you know, and his vein is popping out, and he's got the needle poised and ready to go. Right on the staircase! And there were girls running around the halls in their underwear all last night, and strange guys prowling around and knocking on my door, I'm telling you this is *some* hotel. Which is why I asked if you live here in the city."

"What do you mean?" Carella said, knowing full well what she meant, and *hoping* it was what she meant, and at the same time hoping it was *not* what she meant.

"Like I could go home with you," she said simply, and shrugged.

"Well," Carella said. His mouth was suddenly dry.

"I'm a very big girl," she said, "but I take up very little space, and I promise I'll stay on my side of the bed." She came around to the front of the chair, dropped to her knees, looked up at him, and said, "What do you think?"

The situation seems to be particularly aggravated between three gangs up there—Portoles's gang, which is called The Death's Heads; a black gang called The Scarlet Avengers; and a white gang called The Yankee Rebels.

It's my idea that if I can get them working together on a constructive project, then maybe they'll stop trying to kill each other. I've already made some tentative suggestions along these lines to Portoles, who seems interested in the idea—probably because his closest friend was murdered just six months back, in June. He seems tired of this senseless war. I think he'd like to end it. He also told me that the president of The Scarlet Avengers is a married man with a newborn baby, and really much too old for all this street bopping. It's Portoles's opinion that he might be willing to listen, too.

The real problem may prove to be the president of The Yankee Rebels, who—from all Portoles has told me—is an egotistical, brutal, unforgiving, humorless, puritanical, and basically rather stupid person who has deluded himself into believing he's the only one in the neighborhood who knows the true and righteous path, and that anyone who disagrees with him is either crazy or intent on thwarting his grandiose and thoroughly self-serving schemes. His name is Randall Nesbitt, and I will try to talk to him after I see Portoles tomorrow night, and Atkins, the leader of The Avengers, later in the week.

In the meantime, Golden Girl, I want to get this to the Post Office before it closes. I'll try to write again tomorrow afternoon. Give my love to Choo-Choo. Tell him I hope his sickle is still as shiny bright as always.

Love & peace,
Andy

"Is it any help?" Lisa asked.

He looked down at her. She was still kneeling before him, sitting on her own heels. Her eyes were startlingly blue in the suntanned face.

"Well, actually, we know most of it already. It would have been extremely helpful a few days ago."

"I didn't get it till Thursday."

"Maybe you should have gone to the Los Angeles

cops, after all."

"Then I'd never have got to meet you," she said, and smiled. She put her hand on his knee. "What do you say? Will you take me home?"

"I'm married," he said.

"So what?"

"I don't think my wife would appreciate my taking you home. Even if you *did* stay on your side of the bed."

"I see your point," she said, and smiled again, and he somehow got the idea that she'd been *encouraged* by what he'd just said. And then he wondered whether he'd been *trying* to encourage her, whether he actually *was* toying with the idea of taking blooming, bursting, youthful Lisa Knowles home with him—wherever home might be for the night.

"You wouldn't want to stay here, would you?" she asked.

"No," he said.

"I didn't think so. There were rats running around all last night. One of them even got on the bed. I almost died. Not to mention what was running around in the halls outside. I'll pack," she said, and got to her feet. "It won't take me a minute. We can go someplace else. There are plenty of places in this city, aren't there?"

"Yes, there are plenty of places," he said. "Lisa," he said, "I'm married."

"That's all right," she said, "I don't mind. We don't even have to *do* anything, if you don't want to. I like your face, that's all. I'd like to get to know you better."

"And you'd also like to get out of this fleabag."

"Yes, but that's a secondary consideration. Honestly. What's your name? I know you showed me your badge and told me your name, but I've forgotten it."

"Carella. Steve Carella."

"Steve," she said. "That's a good name. Is the 'Carella' Italian or Spanish or what?"

"Italian."

"That's nice," she said. "That's really nice. Okay? Shall we go someplace?"

"No, I don't think so, Lisa," he said, and rose, and handed her the letter, and then reached into his pocket. From his wallet he took three twenty-dollar bills. "Here," he said.

"What's that?"

"It's enough to buy you a decent room, a good dinner, and a long-distance call to your parents."

"I can't take money from you," she said.

"It's a loan."

"How would I pay you back?"

"I'll give you my address. Pack your bag, okay? I don't want you walking downstairs alone. You can get killed right in the lobby of this joint." He suddenly grinned. "*I'm* almost afraid of going downstairs myself. Here. Take it."

"Thank you," she said, and accepted the money. Quickly, and with great embarrassment, she stuffed the bills into the pocket of her jeans. "Thank you," she said again. "But . . ."

"Yes?"

"Don't think I was . . . I mean . . ." She shrugged. "I wasn't angling for the price of a hotel room, I mean it.

I really *would* like to get to know you. And I've known married men before, so . . . I mean, that wouldn't have mattered. Not to me. But thanks for the money, anyway. I will send it back. Be sure to give me your address."

"I will," Carella said. "Now let's get out of here before I change my mind."

"I wish you would," she said, and grinned.

"Not a chance," he answered.

Nonetheless, he fidgeted uncomfortably all the while she packed, and he rushed her out of the room, and was not able to relax completely until he had put her into a taxi and given the cabbie the name of a small, inexpensive, but legit hotel on the South Side.

He watched the cab as it pulled away from the curb. Lisa wiped condensation from the rear window, and waved through the glass, and the taxi disappeared in a cloud of exhaust fumes.

Carella would not later say to Teddy, "Hey, guess what, honey? A beautiful twenty-two-year-old blonde was flirting with me today, what do you think of that, honey?" Because, somehow, telling that to Teddy would amount to the same thing as having taken Lisa Knowles to bed.

And if he didn't need *one* stupid form of male ego-gratification, he sure as hell didn't need the *other.*

He felt okay.

Swiftly he walked to his automobile through the biting cold. It was beginning to snow.

AT seven-thirty that Monday night, Detective

Charlie Broughan of the 101st made an arrest on his way to work. The arrest was somewhat accidental.

Broughan had come out of the subway kiosk on Concord Avenue, five blocks from the station house, and was walking briskly through the light-falling snow, the pavement already a bit slippery underfoot. A boy and a girl were having what appeared to be a friendly argument on the sidewalk outside a record shop. The boy was wearing a white Swedish Army coat with the familiar insignia of the Death's Heads on it—the black gargoyle with its flaming red tongue. Broughan observed the coat and the insignia with an attitude of weary impatience. So far as he was concerned, there were only good guys and bad guys in the world. Broughan was a good guy, and anybody belonging to the Death's Heads (or *any* of the dumb gangs in this neighborhood) were bad guys. The boy and the girl were talking to each other in Spanish, their voices getting somewhat louder as Broughan approached. Broughan was not looking for trouble, nor was he expecting any. A cop on his way to work doesn't step into sidewalk arguments like Galahad on a white horse. He lets the people yell themselves out, and he continues walking to his office, where slightly more important matters are waiting—like the crazy bastard who was still cutting up prostitutes left and right all over the city, and who was still unidentified, and who only last night had changed his m.o. slightly by *drowning* a hooker in the bathtub of a downtown rathole called the Royal Arms.

"Entonces que hacías en el techo con ella?" the girl asked.

"Yo le estaba enseñando las palomas de Tommy," the boy said.

"Tú estabas tratando de chingarla, eso es lo que tú estabas haciendo," the girl said, and opened her purse.

"No! Solamente le estaba enseñando las palomas," the boy said, and a razor blade suddenly appeared in the girl's right hand, and the blade moved with startling swiftness toward the boy's face, slicing across the bridge of his nose and his right cheek, a gushing trail of blood following the cutting edge as it slashed over the jaw line and almost severed the carotid artery, which would have proved deadly. Blood spilled onto the white Swedish Army coat. The boy, startled, reached into the coat, pulled out a very big gun that Broughan immediately identified as a Colt .45, and pointed it at the girl.

Broughan moved.

He did not say a word. There was no time to pull his own gun. In the next three seconds the cannon in the boy's hand might explode, and Broughan would be dealing with a homicide. The boy had his back to him; Broughan hit him at the base of the skull, with both hands clenched together like a mallet. The boy fell to the sidewalk, barely conscious, and Broughan pulled his gun as the girl began to run. He stuck out his foot, and tripped her, and she went sprawling to the sidewalk, bruising her hands as she tried to cushion the fall. Broughan put them both in handcuffs, told the owner of the record store to call the 101st and tell them Detective Broughan needed a patrol car and a meat wagon, and then turned to the gathering crowd and said, "All right, go home, it's all over."

It was *not* all over. The night was just beginning.

THE boy's name was Pacho Miravitlles.

His face bandaged, he sat on a white table in the emergency room of Washington Hospital and refused to talk to Broughan. While Broughan fired his questions, an intern hovered about, fearful that the boy would begin bleeding again, and maybe die right there on the table, and then *he'd* be somehow blamed for it instead of this big cop who was badgering somebody who'd just been badly injured.

"Why were you carrying that piece?" Broughan said.

Pacho did not answer.

"You're smarter than that, Pacho. You punks never go around heeled unless there's something on. Now what's on, would you like to tell me?"

"Officer," the intern started, and Broughan said, "Shut up," and turned to Pacho again. "Who's the girl?"

"My chick," Pacho answered, apparently figuring this was a safe area for discussion.

"What's her name?"

"Anita Zamora."

"Why'd she cut you?"

"She thought I was fooling around with somebody."

"Who?"

"A girl named Isabel Garrido."

"*Were* you fooling around with her?"

"No. I took her up on the roof to show her my brother's pigeons."

"In this weather?"

"That's what I wanted to show her. The way the pigeons all crowd together in the coop. To keep warm, you know."

"Did she keep *you* warm while you were up there, Pacho?"

"She's only thirteen years old. I wouldn't fool around with nobody that young. I really took her up there to show her the pigeons." He turned to the intern. "Hey, it still feels like blood is under these bandages."

"Officer, I really would like to . . ."

"*I* really would like to find out why this young man was carrying a .45 automatic in the pocket of his coat, Doctor. You've done your job, you stopped the blood, you've got him nicely bandaged there. Now why don't you go outside and have a cigarette, okay?"

"Cigarettes cause cancer," the intern said automatically.

"Then go down to the cafeteria and have a cup of coffee. Or go outside there where you've got a lot of other patients to take care of, okay?"

"This boy is my patient, too."

"I'll take care of this boy, don't you worry about that," Broughan said. "Would you please leave us the hell alone for five minutes?"

"I'm not responsible," the intern said.

"Fine."

"I'm telling you, if anything happens to him, I'm not responsible."

"What do you think is going to happen?"

"He could fall off the table," the intern said.

"He could also slip on the banana peels that are all over the floor."

"What banana peels?"

"There aren't any," Broughan said. "Go take a walk, will you?"

"Okay, but I'm not responsible," the intern said, and walked out.

"What do you say, Pacho?"

"I told you all I got to tell you."

"Tell me about the piece."

"No comment."

"You got a license to carry that weapon?"

"You know I ain't got no license."

"Okay, so to begin with, we got you on a gun charge. You know what else we got you on?"

"You got me on nothing."

"You're mistaken, Pacho. We got you on a couple of things that are very interesting. You were holding a loaded weapon in your hand, and you were pointing it at your nice little girl friend who already cut you up, and who's going to be charged with First-Degree Assault. We can charge you with the same thing, at the very least, since—"

"The gun in my hand don't mean nothing."

"Uh-uh, it means a *lot*, Pacho. It means you violated Section 240 of the Penal Law. You assaulted another person with a loaded firearm."

"I never touched her. I never fired a shot."

"You stuck the gun in her face. We can presume you intended firing it. But Assault is the least of your worries, Pacho. We might decide to charge you with Attempted Homicide instead. That's an even heavier rap."

"I didn't try to kill nobody. I only wanted to scare her. Anyway, it was self-defense."

"Yeah, well, let's not try the case right here and now, okay, Pacho? I'm just trying to tell you how much time you're going to *absolutely* spend in jail, and how much time you *might* spend in jail if a jury sees it the same way the D.A. sees it. On the gun charge, you'll absolutely and without question get a year for carrying a loaded firearm without a license. On the assault, you can get ten years, and on the attempted murder, you can get twenty-five. How old are you, Pacho?"

"Nineteen."

"Either way, by the time you get out of prison, you won't be a teen-ager any more. How does that appeal to you?"

"It don't."

"So tell me why you were carrying that piece."

"Go fuck yourself," Pacho said.

BERT KLING was about to propose to Augusta Blair.

It was almost nine-thirty, and they had finished their meal and their coffee, and Kling had ordered cognac for both of them, and they were waiting for it to arrive.

There was a candle in a red translucent holder on the tabletop, and it cast a gentle glow on Augusta's face, softening her features, not that she needed any help. There was a time when Kling had been thoroughly flustered by Augusta's beauty. In her presence he had been speechless, breathless, awkward, stupid, and incapable of doing anything but stare at her in wonder and gratitude. Over the past nine months, however, he had not only grown accustomed to her beauty, and comfortable in its presence, but had also begun to feel somehow responsible for it—like the curator of a museum beginning to think that the rare paintings on the walls had not only been discovered by him, but had in fact been *painted* by him.

If Kling had been a painter, he would have put Augusta on canvas exactly the way she looked, no improvements, no embellishments; none were necessary. Augusta's hair was red, or auburn, or russet, depending on the light, but certainly in the red spectrum, and worn long most of the time, usually falling to just below her shoulder blades, but sometimes worn back in a pony tail, or braided into pigtails on either side of her face, or even piled on top of her head like a crown of sparkling rubies. Her eyes were a jade-green, slanting upward from high cheekbones, her exquisite nose gently drawing the upper lip away from partially exposed, even white teeth. She was tall and slender, with good breasts and a narrow waist and wide hips and splendid wheels. She was surely the most beautiful woman he had ever met in his life—which is why she was a photographer's model. She was also the most beautiful *person* he had ever met in his life—which is why he wanted to marry her.

"Augusta," he said, "there's something serious I'd like to ask you."

"Yes, Bert?" she said, and looked directly into his face, and he felt again what he had first felt nine months ago when he'd walked into her burglarized apartment and seen her sitting on the couch, her eyes glistening with tears about to spill. He had clumsily shaken hands with her, and his heart had stopped.

"I've been doing a lot of thinking," he said.

"Yes, Bert?" she said.

The waiter brought the cognac. Augusta lifted her snifter and rolled it between her palms. Kling picked up his snifter and almost dropped it, spilling some of the cognac onto the tablecloth. He dabbed at it with his napkin, smiled weakly at Augusta, put the napkin back on his lap and the snifter back on the table before he spilled it all over his shirt and his pants and the rug and maybe the silk-brocaded walls of this very fancy French joint he had chosen because he thought it would be a suitably romantic setting for a proposal, even though it was costing him half-a-week's pay. "Augusta," he said, and cleared his throat.

"Yes, Bert?"

"Augusta, I have something very serious to ask you."

"Yes, Bert, you've said that already." There seemed to be a slight smile on her mouth. Her eyes looked exceedingly merry.

"Augusta?"

"Yes, Bert?"

"Excuse me, Mr. Kling," the waiter said. "There's a telephone call for you."

"Oh, sh—" Kling started, and then nodded, and said, "Thank you, thank you." He shoved his chair back, dropping his napkin to the floor as he rose. He picked up the napkin, said, "Excuse me, Augusta," and was heading away from the table when she very softly said, "Bert?"

He stopped and turned.

"I will, Bert," she said.

"You will?" he asked.

"I'll marry you," she said.

"Okay," he said, and smiled. "I'll marry you, too."

"Okay," she said.

"Okay," he said.

He walked swiftly across the room. The waiter regarded him curiously, because he had never seen a man looking so completely ecstatic over the mere prospect of answering a telephone. Kling closed the door of the booth, waggled his fingers at Augusta across the room, waited for her to waggle her fingers back at him, and then said, "Hello?"

"Bert, this is Steve. I tried to get you at home, your service gave me this number."

"Yeah, Steve, what's up?"

"You'd better get up here right away," Carella said. "All hell is breaking loose."

9

As the president, I make it my business to know everything that's going on every place. From the wire we had in the Scarlets' clubhouse on Gateside, we found out exactly where they were keeping Big and Jo-Jo prisoner. The idea, of course, was to free them. But that wasn't enough. It was also necessary to punish the Scarlets for what they done.

I want to make something clear. You guys are writing this down, and you're also taping it, and so I want to make it clear. It's not always easy to understand why a person does such and such a thing. You look at the externals, and you think Oh, he done that for selfish reasons, or Oh, he done it out of spite, or because he lost his temper, or whatever. You can come up with a thousand speculations as to why a person done something, when actually it's only the person himself who knows why. So I want to tell you exactly why I done it, and I also want to make sure you know *what* I done and what I *didn't* do.

You found me with blood all over my hands tonight. Okay, that doesn't necessarily mean anything. I can tell you with absolute honesty that I never killed nobody. I can also tell you that although I ordered the raids that ended the war once and for all—and don't forget I *did* end the war, the war *is* over, there's never going to be no more trouble in this neighborhood—it was not me personally who did any of the killing. No matter what it looked like (and I admit my hands were covered with blood), evidence can be misleading lots of times, as I'm sure you guys know. And if you look at just the blood, then you can forget the very real things I accomplished. That's the reason I'm telling you all this. You think I don't know you can't force me to say anything I don't want to? I'm telling you all this because I want to set the record straight. I don't want you to forget what I done. I don't want you to lose sight of the forest for the trees.

The place they were holding Big and Jo-Jo was in the cellar of this candy store on Gatsby and 51st. The candy store is owned by this guy called Lamp Hawkins. He's a nigger who lost his eye in a street fight back in the fifties, some guy stabbed him in the eye. He used to live in Diamondback, and the gangs down there were rumbling all the time back in those days, but very unsophisticated, low-level combat, you understand? Like they used zip guns and ripped-off car aerials and switchblades, and they used to throw bricks down from the rooftops. Kid stuff. When you compare that to the weaponry we got today, but which we always use with restraint, it's almost laughable. Because the point is, you see, you can go to jail for carrying a homemade piece in your pocket, so you might as well carry the real thing, am I right? I want to point out, by the way, that I wasn't carrying *nothing* when you picked me up. You did not find no firearm on my person, and don't forget it.

Anyway, this Lamp character moved up from Diamondback after he got out of jail for pushing dope, and he opened this candy store on Gatsby, which is really a front for a numbers drop. I guess you guys already know that. He probably pays you off, don't he? And the reason he let the Scarlets bring two prisoners there was that he needed their clique for protection. Against *us,* you dig? Because he knew the one thing the Yankee Rebels cannot abide is anything that has to do with dope. Now, you may say that Lamp got picked up for pushing 'way back in the sixties, and he done his time and paid the penalty, but that's not good enough for me. I got a memory like an elephant. Once a guy has pushed dope on innocent little children, you can bet he will one day or another go right back to pushing again. Which is why this clique shows no mercy whatsoever to anybody who is involved with dope on any level—using, dealing, we don't care what. One of our club rules is no junk and no junkies. That is an ironclad rule. No junk and no junkies. So Lamp lived in fear of his life all the time because he knew if we ever caught him out in the open, we would do to him what he done to countless little children back in the sixties. We would ruin him. And that's why he let Mighty Man bring the two prisoners to the candy store and lock them in the cellar. He was taking a chance, sure, but it was a worse chance for him to walk the streets without Scarlet protection.

I spent all afternoon today doping out a plan of attack.

Toy gave me a lot of support, I have to say that. She is a tireless person. She sets a fine example for the other girls in the clique. She is such a lady. And this afternoon, when I was figuring out the raids, talking out loud to myself most of the time, Toy was there to ask if I needed a cup of coffee, or if I would like her to do the back of my neck (she massages my neck whenever I get these tension headaches), and just generally lending me support. By about four o'clock I had figured out what I thought was a good plan, and whereas I would not normally have called the council for their opinion, this was a matter of great importance to the clique and to the entire neighborhood. So I put it to them.

The most important thing, I told them, was to get the prisoners back, and nothing should be done to jeopardize their safe return. I figured that a frontal attack on the candy store was the best approach here, since Big and Jo-Jo were in the cellar and could not possibly be harmed by any shooting that was done upstairs. We were not concerned for our own safety, as we intended to go in there heavily armed, and we also had the element of surprise on our side. We had been in that candy store once or twice before, risking capture or bodily harm from the Scarlets, but eager to tell Mr. Lamp Hawkins that if we so much as saw him walking on the street alone at any time of the day or night, we would string him up from a lamppost. On those occasions we didn't risk actually *doing* anything to Lamp while we were in Scarlet territory because that would have caused an escalation of the war we were trying so hard to end.

The layout of the candy store was very simple. On a wooden stand outside, Lamp kept his newspapers. Just inside the door, on the left, there was a rack with magazines and paperback books, most of them dirty porn stuff, which was another good reason for giving Lamp the full treatment if the opportunity ever presented itself. Opposite that was the counter, with stools in front of it, and ice cream bins and soda spigots and everything behind it. There was a door at the far end of the store, and we figured it led to the back room where Lamp lived and where the numbers drop was. We also figured there must be another door back there that led to the cellar. So the plan was to go right in blasting, get rid of Lamp on the spot and be careful not to harm any innocent bystanders in the store. The raiders would go in the back room, find the door to the basement, kick it in because it would probably be locked, and get rid of any Scarlets who were there guarding Big and Jo-Jo. I figured we needed a force of no more than four good men to take the candy store.

Mace, my war counselor, suggested that we go in with hand grenades, taking out the front of the store without any risk. The council voted, and it was decided that two men would throw in the grenades (we have sixty-four grenades in our arsenal, but they are getting more and more difficult to come by) and they would be backed by two more men, if in case something went wrong—like maybe Lamp or somebody in the store tossing the grenades out again, you know what I mean? In which case, the four would just go in and shoot up the place. In other words, Plan A would be blowing up the front of the store and then running back and down to the cellar. Plan B, in case the grenades failed, was to go in shooting.

But that wasn't all of it. It seemed to me that there was only one way to end this war once and for all, and that was to completely annihilate the enemy. I told the council that by the enemy I didn't mean only the Scarlets, who were holding our men prisoner. I meant the Heads as well, that the thing to do since they had not learned their lesson of a week ago when we staged the double-hit was to move in fast and wipe them out to the last man. I knew this was a drastic measure, but I reasoned with the council that if there is nobody left to fight a war, then the war automatically stops.

One of the kids on the council, a dope named Hardy, said he didn't understand why we were fighting this war to *begin* with, and I told him the war wasn't our doing, but that as the most powerful clique in the neighborhood, if not the entire city, it was our duty and our responsibility to bring peace, even though we hadn't started the shooting. I also reminded him of what had happened to a former Yankee Rebel named Jonathan Quince, who had started questioning the way things were run, and Hardy right away apologized and said he wasn't questioning nothing, he was simply wondering out loud, since the war seemed to have been going on for as long as he could remember, practically from when he was a kid in diapers. I told Hardy that the reason the war hadn't ended till now was because I hadn't been president.

So Hardy, the dope, tells me in front of everybody that this is my second term as president, and if I had all these ideas about ending the war, why didn't I do it in my first term, end the war right then and there, without more bloodshed and killing? He was beginning to sound like Johnny all over again, but I kept my cool, I did not blow up. There were important things we were about to do, and I couldn't waste time dealing with a jerk. I just reminded him that the enemy was intransigent, which was why I had finally decided to take drastic measures. Then I told him to shut up and listen for a change, and maybe he might learn something. He started to say something else, and Chingo rapped him right in the mouth, and that was the end of Hardy's little private protest.

Following the raid on the candy store, I told the council that I wished to hit the clubhouse of the Scarlets and the clubhouse of the Heads. I told them that I wished these to be full-scale attacks, with a large part of our membership involved, and that as commander in chief I personally would lead the raid on the Scarlet clubhouse, as I was anxious to confront Mighty Man, who had told me the obscenity on the telephone. I told the council that I wished there to be nothing left of the Scarlets or the Heads by the time we got finished with them tonight. I told them we had given both those clubs ample opportunity to negotiate, but they had refused to accept our kindnesses and our compromises, and so now it was time to quit kidding around, it was time to destroy their capability for waging war, and therefore to end the war itself in that way. I also mentioned, and I sincerely meant this, that I hoped tonight would mark the last of the killing and the bloodshed, that perhaps from now on we could walk the streets of this neighborhood without fear, and that we could do so with pride, knowing that we had not compromised our honor. I think the council was moved. They voted eleven-to-one to carry out my plan as I had conceived it, and then The Bullet suggested that the man who had voted against it (Hardy, of course) change his vote to make it unanimous, and he did so without no further urgings.

The hit on the candy store was scheduled for nine-thirty.

We figured that after we got Big and Jo-Jo back, the Scarlets would call a meeting in their clubhouse to discuss how they were going to deal with this new development. We knew from past experience that they could move very fast when they wanted to, and we figured they would be assembled by ten, and that a safe time to hit the Gateside building would be ten-thirty. So that was the zero hour for the second hit.

As for the Heads, we planned to hit them with a sep-arate force at exactly the same time, ten-thirty, on the assumption that news of the increased hostilities between the Scarlets and us would cause them also to call a meeting, and we would catch them all together in their rathole clubhouse with four-eyed Henry pre-siding, and that would be the end of the whole confla-gration.

We did not know at the time that the Heads had plans of their own.

It was the Heads who messed everything up.

PATROLMAN **F**RANCISCUS of the 101st was

riding shotgun in the r.m.p. car when he and the driver, Patrolman Jenkins, heard the blast. It had begun snowing more heavily, and they had pulled to the curb not twenty minutes before to put skid chains on the car. But Jenkins instinctively hit the brake when he heard the explosion, and despite the chains, the car's tail whipped sharply to the left, and he swore, and turned into the skid, and then said to Franciscus, "What the hell was that?"

"I don't know," Franciscus said. He had been listening to the incessant squawk of the car radio, and had been half asleep. He looked at his watch. It was only nine-thirty; his tour would not end till eleven forty-five. Two hours and fifteen minutes to go, and now maybe a busted gas main or something, which meant they would have to get out of the car in this damn freezing weather and start handling crowds and traffic.

"Sounds like it came from around the corner," Jenkins said.

"Yeah," Franciscus said.

"You know what it sounded like?"

"Yeah, a gas main."

"No. It sounded like when I was with the Third Precinct downtown, this boiler went up in the basement of a diner on the corner. It knocked the whole front wall out of the building. That's what this sounded like."

"I think it sounded like a gas main," Franciscus said, and shrugged.

"Well, let's take a look," Jenkins said, and turned

on the siren.

The candy store was a smoldering wreck when they pulled up to the curb. Franciscus sighed; this was going to be worse than a gas main. Jenkins was already on the car radio, telling the dispatcher who answered his call that this was a 10-66. When he was asked to specify, he said there'd been an explosion in a candy store at 1155 Gatsby, cause undetermined. As Franciscus got out of the car, a black man with a patch over his right eye staggered from the candy store. His clothes were smoking, punctuated with a dozen bleeding wounds that gave his shirt a red-polka-dot effect. The flesh on his face hung from his cheeks and jaw in tattered trailing ribbons. As he stumbled toward the curb he brought up his left hand, presumably to wipe blood out of his one good eye, and then suddenly collapsed to the sidewalk. Franciscus said "Jesus," and yelled to Jenkins that they'd need a meat wagon, and then went into the candy store.

The floor was covered with paperback books and magazines, broken glasses and dishes, utensils twisted out of shape. The supporting pedestals of the counter stools had been bent almost double by the explosion, so that they resembled giant blackened toadstools ravaged by a storm. The mirror behind the counter had been shattered, and shards lay over the blistered counter top and on the floor behind the counter, where they lay submerged in a soupy mixture of ice cream and syrup. A partially naked teen-aged girl was standing leaning against the wall at the far end of the room, where a jagged, splintered door stood open and hanging on one hinge. Most of her clothing had been ripped off in the blast, and she stood with bleeding breasts and arms, panties torn to shreds, one shoe on her left foot, leaning against the wall, staring sightlessly at Franciscus as he came into the shop.

He went to her swiftly, and said, "It's all right, miss, we're getting an ambulance," and he took her arm to guide her out of the store, just gently closing his fingers around the elbow, and the girl fell away from the wall, face forward onto the floor, and Franciscus realized she was dead, and that he was still holding her arm, even though the girl was lying at his feet. His eyes opened wide in recognition, he dropped the severed arm, and turned away from the girl, turned his face into the corner where the door hung on its single hinge, and puked into his cupped hands.

Outside, Jenkins was on the radio ordering the ambulance when he saw six boys in blue denim jackets running out of the alley that led to the back of the store. As they came out of the alley and started up the avenue, he saw that the backs of their jackets were decorated with Confederate flags. He got out of the car, revolver in hand, and yelled, "Police officer, halt!" but the six boys were moving swiftly toward the corner, and did not stop. "Hey!" he yelled again. "You hear me?" and fired a warning shot in the air. The boys did not stop. They rounded the corner and disappeared from sight. Jenkins got back into the car and told the dispatcher, "We got six suspects, fleeing north on Toland, all of them wearing Yankee Rebel jackets."

Then he went into the candy store, and found Franciscus standing in the corner of the room, the dead girl at his feet, his hands stinking of vomit and covering his face. Franciscus was crying. Jenkins had never seen a cop crying in all his years on the force.

"Hey," he said, "come on, Ralphie."

But Franciscus could not stop crying.

CARELLA did not reach the 101st in Riverhead until a few minutes past ten. By that time Patrolman Jenkins's radio call had resulted in the street capture, four blocks away, of the Yankee Rebels he had seen running from the scene of the candy-store explosion. The six youths were gathered in the Interrogation Room of the 101st now, slouching in straight-backed chairs around the long wooden table. Charlie Broughan needed a shave; Carella suddenly wondered if he *ever* shaved.

"You I know, and you I know," Broughan said, pointing to two of the boys. "This is Big Anthony Sutherland," he said to Carella, "and this is Jo-Jo Cottrell."

"I've been looking for you," Carella said.

"Yeah?" Big Anthony replied, and shrugged. He was an enormous young man, with huge shoulders and a weight lifter's pectorals bulging against the blue shirt he wore under the denim jacket. Casually bored, he brushed a hank of long blond hair off his forehead.

"You've been out of town, I guess."

Big Anthony shrugged again.

"Who're you four?" Broughan asked the other boys. None of them answered. "Your names," he said.

"Go ahead, tell them," Big Anthony said.

"I'm Priest," one of the boys said.

"Your *full* names, never mind the gang shit," Broughan said.

"Mark Priestley."

"And you?"

"Charles Ingersol."

"Well, well, we got us a *big* fish, huh?" Broughan said. "We got ourselves Chingo in person, the enforcement officer of the Yankee Rebels."

"That's me," Chingo said.

"And you?"

"Peter Hastings."

"How about you?" he asked the last of the six.

"Frank Hughes."

"Okay, boys, what were you doing running from the back of that candy store?"

None of the boys answered.

"I'll direct this all to you, Chingo, okay?" Broughan said. "Since you're such a big man in the organization."

"Better tell me my rights first," Chingo said.

"What for? Did you do something?"

"Nothing at all."

"Then why do you need to know your rights? Which you probably know already anyway."

"I got a bad memory," Chingo said. "Tell me again."

"We're not charging you with anything, we're only soliciting information regarding a crime," Broughan said.

"Ah, excuse me, Charlie," Carella said politely, "but

shouldn't we handle that matter for the Turman police first?"

"Why, certainly, Steve," Broughan said, "go right ahead."

"Thank you," Carella said, smiling, and then the smile dropped from his face, and he pointed his finger at Big Anthony and said, "You."

"Me?"

"You."

"Don't point, it's impolite."

"The police in Turman have a warrant out for your arrest. They've authorized us to pick you up and question you regarding the murder of one Margaret McNally last Thursday night. You can consider yourself under arrest as of right this minute."

"If the police in Turman want me, they better extradite me," Big Anthony said.

"First things first," Carella answered. "You feel like answering some questions? This may all be a big mistake, and maybe we can clear it up in ten minutes. If it *is* a mistake, I'll call the Turman cops and tell them you're clean. What do you say?"

"I don't feel like answering no questions."

"Well, just in case you change your mind, and in keeping with the Supreme Court decision in *Miranda v. Arizona,* I'm informing you now that we are not permitted to ask you any questions until you are warned of your right to counsel and your privilege against self-incrimination."

"You're goddamn right," Big Anthony said.

"Since I *would* like to ask you some questions—"

"Save your breath."

"—I'm now telling you that, first, you have the right to remain silent if you so desire. Do you understand that?"

"Sure."

"Second, you don't have to answer any questions if you don't want to."

"The same goes for the rest of you punks, so you might as well listen," Broughan said.

"Do you understand that?"

"Yeah, yeah," Big Anthony said.

"How about the rest of you?"

The other boys mumbled or nodded assent.

"Third," Carella said, "if you *do* decide to answer any questions . . ."

"I told you—"

"Shut up and listen to the man," Broughan said.

"That's already a violation of my rights," Big Anthony said.

"Where'd you get your law degree?" Broughan said.

"I don't need a law degree to—"

"Shut your fuckin' mouth and listen to the man," Broughan said.

"If you *do* decide to answer any questions," Carella said, "the answers may be used as evidence against you. Do you understand that?"

"This is a waste of time."

"*Do* you understand it?"

"Yeah, yeah."

"And you also have the right to consult with an attorney before or during questioning. If you don't have money to hire a lawyer, we'll appoint one for you."

"What the hell are you telling me all this crap for?" Big Anthony said.

"Because this is a democracy," Broughan answered dryly.

"I ain't going to answer no questions, anyway."

"You may decide to, who knows?" Broughan said. "Freedom of choice, that's what the whole system's about."

"Yeah, bullshit," Big Anthony said.

"And lastly," Carella said, "if you *do* decide to answer any questions, with or without a lawyer present, you can stop any time you want to. Is that also clear?"

"It's all clear. I got nothing to say."

"Fine. We're holding you for the Turman police either way."

"I don't even *know* anybody named Margaret whatever-the-hell."

"The Turman cops have a witness who saw you in the woods off Route 14 last Thursday night. The girl's body was at your feet, and the witness overheard you arguing with another boy about whether or not to bury her."

"Prove it."

"Oh, I'm sure we will. Or *they* will. Or *somebody* will. With so many law-enforcement agencies involved, you're in pretty hot water. Anyway, if you've got nothing to say, that's that. Charlie, can we get somebody to take him down for booking and detention?"

"Oh, sure," Broughan said, and reached for the phone on the corner of the table.

"There's only *two* agencies involved," Big Anthony said.

"Until the FBI gets into it," Carella said.

"Why would *they* get into it? You said—"

"Oh, I think the Turman cops have some idea the girl was kidnapped and transported across a state line. That's enough to bring in the FBI automatically. Pretty heavy stuff, Anthony. Killing a kidnap victim."

"Hello, Mike, we got somebody we need booked and iced," Broughan said into the phone. "Send a patrolman up, will you?" He listened a moment, and then said, "A warrant from the Turman police. Kidnap and homicide. No, we won't need a stenographer 'cause he don't want to make a statement. Right, thank you, Mike." Broughan replaced the receiver on its cradle, turned to Carella and said, "Done. You think we should talk to these other young gentlemen now? Regarding the double homicide at the candy store on Gatsby?"

The other young gentlemen had listened in somewhat awed stupefaction to the conversation between Carella and Big Anthony, and were now being made aware that it was *their* turn again. The attitude of the two cops was so matter-of-fact, so thoroughly bland, so *real* that it conversely generated an aura of unreality in the small, windowless Interrogation Room. Each of the boys (and especially Big Anthony, who had just been told what serious trouble he was in) was unprepared for this impersonal, antiseptic approach, and felt totally dehumanized by it. There was no saying Hey, listen, you guys, we were acting on orders, you know? Like this has nothing to do with murder. This is just stuff between the cliques. In fact, we're about to settle it, if you'll just let us alone.

Uh-uh. These cops were businessmen talking calmly and coolly about crimes committed, and about the penalties for those crimes, and about the various law-enforcement agencies who were going to make sure somebody *paid* those penalties. One of the boys, Charles "Chingo" Ingersol, the powerful and highly respected enforcement officer of the Yankee Rebels, suddenly discovered that he had an irresistible urge to urinate, and he only hoped he would not wet his pants in front of the other guys. He debated asking the cops whether he could go down the hall to the bathroom. But he was sure they would refuse. They were hard-headed businessmen, and they weren't about to waste company time on somebody running down the hall to pee. Chingo was scared. All of them were scared. And both Carella and Broughan knew it.

"Chingo," Broughan said, and the boy visibly started when his name was announced that way.

"Yeah," he said, trying to affect his normal cool, even though an uncontrollable twitch had started in his lower left eyelid.

"You want to tell us what happened at the candy store?"

"Nothing happened."

"Looked like a hell of a mess to me."

"Yeah, somebody must've done something there,"

Chingo said. "But it wasn't us."

"Then how come you were running out of the alleyway?"

"We were shooting crap back there when we heard the police siren. So we split, that's all."

"Oh, you were shooting crap, I see," Broughan said.

"That's it."

"In the dark?"

"Well . . . we had a flashlight."

"Where is it?"

"Where's what?"

"The flashlight."

"We must've dropped it when we split."

"You were shooting crap in an alley behind a candy store in Scarlet Avenger territory, is that what you're asking us to believe?"

"Yeah."

"Yankee Rebels casually shooting crap in—"

"They didn't know we were there," Chingo said.

The door to the Interrogation Room opened. A patrolman looked into the room, took a pair of hand-cuffs from his belt, and cheerfully said, "Who's the customer?"

"The big one there," Broughan said.

"Let's go, fella," the patrolman said, and walked to Big Anthony, and closed the jagged, saw-toothed jaws of one handcuff over his right wrist. "Your mother must feed you pretty good," the patrolman said. "How tall are you, anyway?"

"Six-four."

"You're a healthy kid," the patrolman said. "Let's

go, the sergeant wants to see you."

"I didn't do nothing," Big Anthony said to the patrolman.

"I know, I know," the patrolman said understandingly. "Nobody *ever* done nothing."

"I don't even know the girl," Big Anthony said.

"That makes us even," the patrolman said. "*I* don't know her, either."

"Look, whyn't you tell these guys . . . ?"

"Me? I just work here," the patrolman said. "You tell them yourself."

"They think I killed somebody."

"Well, if you didn't kill anybody, it'll all be cleared up. Meantime, you come on downstairs 'cause the sergeant's got a few questions he wants to ask you, and he also wants to write your name in the big book. Okay?" He turned to Broughan. "Has he been advised?"

"He has, but tell Mike to go through it again."

"Who we holding him for?"

"The Turman police. And most likely the Feebs."

"Right," the patrolman said, and jerked on the handcuff. "Let's go."

The other Yankee Rebels watched as Big Anthony was led silently out of the room. The frosted-glass door to the Interrogation Room closed.

"Fellow named Lucas Hawkins was killed in the blast," Broughan said to Chingo. "Called himself 'Lamp.' Had one eye. Ever recall seeing him around?"

"No," Chingo said.

"Little girl got killed, too. I guess she was browsing

the magazine rack, or maybe just sitting at the counter when somebody threw the bomb in. Thirteen-year-old kid. Her name was Daisy Cooper. That's a nice name, don't you think?"

"Yeah," Chingo said.

"Daisy Cooper. She was dead on arrival. Lamp died on the way to the hospital. Very heavy stuff, that bombing. Want to tell us about it?"

"Nothing to say," Chingo whispered.

"What? Speak up, son."

"I . . ." Chingo cleared his throat and raised his voice. "I said I got nothing to say."

"Well, fine, that's up to you. Any of you other guys?"

The other Yankee Rebels looked at each other searchingly, and then looked at Chingo, and then shook their heads.

"Fine," Broughan said. "We'll have to lock all of you up, you understand, till we get to the bottom of this. But we got nice clean detention cells downstairs, with little potties in them and everything. You'll have very nice bowel movements while you're here at the 101st. Steve, you want to ask anything?"

"I just wanted to mention that our eyewitness'll certainly be able to identify whoever was with Anthony on the night of the murder. It might go easier—well, I can't make any promises."

"No, you can't do that, Steve."

"I know, I'm merely saying if any of the boys here happened to be with Anthony that night, I'd appreciate him stepping forward now."

Nobody stepped forward.

"I didn't think so," Carella said, and sighed. "Well, I guess you fellows know what you're doing, but you're sure making it difficult for yourselves. Let's get somebody to take them down, huh, Charlie?"

"Yeah, we'd better do that," Broughan said, and was reaching for the telephone when it rang. He lifted the receiver. "Broughan," he said, and listened. "Where?" He looked up at the wall clock. The time was 10:25. "Okay," Broughan said, "I'm on my way."

"What is it?" Carella asked.

"World War III," Broughan answered.

WE were coming down Gateside, we were almost to the corner where the Scarlets have their clubhouse. Gateside and Delaney. There were twenty of us. I was in the lead. Mace, at the same time, was leading an attack on the Heads' clubhouse on Concord and Forty-eighth. It was all synchronized. It all should have worked beautiful.

Let me explain that we weren't tiptoeing around, we weren't ducking in hallways, we were marching right down the middle of the street. We planned to surprise the Scarlets, sure, but we weren't dumb enough to think we could sneak *up* on them. They got sentries and runners the same as us. We knew they had their arsenal far away from the clubhouse, though, just the way we do. That's so if the fuzz come around, there's no gun charge to pin on anybody. Just a bunch of guys sitting around rapping, that's all. You can't arrest nobody for rapping. So we knew they didn't have guns up there, and we figured even if the runners *did* get to them, they'd maybe have three minutes' notice that we were almost on them, and three minutes wasn't enough time to get out of that building and escape what was coming. Which was us. The Yankee Rebels. Thirty-four strong, and marching down that street with our colors proudly showing—red, white, and blue on the move. With another twenty of us over on Concord Avenue about to end the war with the Heads at the same time.

There was only one trouble.

The Heads weren't on Concord Avenue.

The Heads were on Gateside.

And what the Heads were planning to do was wipe out the Scarlets, and then come after us, and that way become undisputed rulers of the whole neighborhood.

It was The Bullet who spotted those white Swedish Army coats up the block. It was hard to see them at first, because it was snowing hard, and the streets were already covered, and those coats were pretty effective camouflage. But The Bullet has very sharp eyes. He can see in the dark like a cat, and not even white-against-white can faze him. He grabs my arm, and he tells me to take a look up the block, and all I can see at first is this swirling snow, and then through the snow I see what looks like a moving snowbank, you know what I mean? Only it ain't a snowbank, it's maybe a dozen guys all dressed in white coats, and I realize all at once it's a party of Heads coming right for us on a collision course.

The first thing I thought was that Mace hit early, and

that his force got wiped out. But that ain't like Mace. We had set our watches before we started out, and Mace knew both strike forces were supposed to hit at ten-thirty sharp. It was now only ten twenty-five, and if I knew Mace, he was looking at his watch right then and timing his strike to the second. The only trouble was that all the Heads were *here* instead of where Mace expected them to be.

I always think best under pressure.

I have had maybe six important crisises in my life, and I have always met them and solved them. This was just another crisis, no different from the other ones. This was a football team coming down the field, armed to the teeth, but only another ball club. I had the stronger team, and we were going to beat them and end this war. All it involved was a change of plan. Instead of the Scarlets and the Heads simultaneously, it would have to be the Heads first, right there in the street, and *then* the Scarlets.

I gave the order to charge.

It was very exciting. I had, well, an erection. I don't know why.

We met in the middle of the street. Intelligence had told me the Heads had a very good armory, but I didn't expect the kind of opposition we got from them. Their weaponry was very sophisticated. I'd always suspected they were brothers with a clique in Calm's Point, and the stuff they were using against us now led me to believe they were being supplied by this other clique. Otherwise, where would they have got the stuff they threw at us? In spite of their heavy hardware, though, we had them outnumbered, and in the first three minutes after we joined battle, there must've been six or seven of them laying in the middle of the street, bleeding all over their nice white coats.

But I should've realized something was wrong from the minute The Bullet spotted them. There weren't *enough* of them. If this was a full-scale raid on the Scarlet clubhouse, why were the Heads throwing only a dozen men at them? We ourselves had come down the street with thirty-four guys. Was it possible the Heads had underestimated the strength of the Scarlets? No, it wasn't possible. Their intelligence was as good as ours, and they must've known the Scarlets were a very strong club. So why the small attack force?

The answer to that one came as a total surprise, though now that I think of it, it was really very good military planning. I always give credit where credit is due, and if the Heads planned a good attack, I'll say so, plain and honest. It was a flanking attack, you see. They were going to hit the building from two sides. The first group, the one we met in the street on Gateside Avenue, was obviously supposed to go in the front door of the building. The second group, the one that came down Delaney Street was, I guess, supposed to go in the side basement door to the building. But what happened was they saw us engaged with the main attack force on Gateside, and the next thing you knew we were caught in a pincers, fighting with the Gateside group in front of us and the Delaney group behind us. It was bad news. There was only one thing we could do, and even that was risky, but we did it, anyway. We ran in the building.

The Bullet and six of our guys covered our rear, holing up in the entryway and firing out into the street, keeping the Heads away while the rest of us charged up the stairs to get the Scarlets. The first Scarlet we met was a little nigger punk named Jeremy Atkins, who was a junior and the brother of Lewis Atkins, who we had done away with the week before. He was coming down the stairs, probably to see what all the noise was in the street outside, and Little Anthony cut him down with three fast shots, and he came falling headfirst down the stairs, and we all got out of the way to let him go by, and Doc gave him a kick in the ribs when he come to a stop about ten steps from the bottom.

Mighty Man himself was standing at the top of the steps.

I was not armed, you know, I have already told you that. I know you don't believe me, but that's the absolute truth, I was not armed. It was not me who killed Mighty Man. I don't know who did it. Whoever did it was a very good shot. Two bullets took Mighty Man right between the eyes, one bullet right over the other, bang, bang, two neat little holes drilled right between his eyes, it was beautiful. He fell dead on the spot, and we climbed over him and ran into this big room they got up there, smelling of nigger sweat and piss, and all the guys were scrambling and realizing this was a raid and they were about to get wiped out. Doc took a bullet just when I heard the sirens. He took a bullet in the gut. Everybody was shooting and yelling, and beginning to run out of the place because they knew sirens meant fuzz, and this was designed to end the war, not to get busted and rot in jail. People were climbing all over me. Doc tried to get up. He was holding his guts together. Somebody had shot him with a very big caliber gun, probably a .45, those niggers like big guns. He fell against me, and I tried to hold him up, but he was slippery and wet, and my hands got all covered with blood, and that's when I heard somebody downstairs yelling, "Police officer, hold it right there!" and that's when you guys came up, and put handcuffs on me, and brought me here.

So when you ask me why I did it, I got some questions to ask *you* right back. The first question is why I did *what?* Why I tried to bring peace to the neighborhood? Why I tried to end this war that's been going on between the cliques for God knows how long? Why I tried to solve it with honor and with pride? Why I tried to rid the streets of two cliques who were a danger to maybe the whole city? If that is the question you're asking, then the answer is like I said before.

I did it because I'm the president, that's why. I'm the elected leader, and it is my duty and my responsibility to take care of the people I am serving.

That's all there is to it. That's all I got to say.

THEY led Randall Nesbitt out of the squadroom in handcuffs. He walked with his head high, that peculiar television-personality smile on his mouth. At the end of the corridor he turned and gave a short chopping wave of his hand to the detectives who were watching him.

"He *still* doesn't know what he did," Kling said.

"He never *will* know," Carella answered.

"The jury'll remind him."

"Yes. Thank God there are still juries."

Meyer Meyer, who had passed Nesbitt and his police escort on the steps outside, came into the squadroom now, took off his hat and coat, and said, "Who was that?"

"That was the president," Carella said. "We've got a whole cageful of his people downstairs. And Broughan up at the 101st has two other gangs locked up. Too many of them to fit in one station house."

"Yeah?" Meyer said. "What'd he do?"

"He ended the war," Carella said.

"Where're *you* coming from?" Kling asked.

"Me? I just got taken to dinner by a writer."

"Dinner?" Kling said, looking up at the clock. It was twenty minutes past eleven.

"Dinner, yes. In a very fancy restaurant. And then we took a walk up Hall Avenue while I told him my views on the relationship of television to acts of violence."

"What'd you tell him?" Carella asked.

"I told him there are worse influences in this country than television. I told him if anybody needed violent heroes to imitate, he could find plenty of them around without ever turning on a television set."

"Who did you have in mind?" Carella asked.